"Say yes."

It was insane. It was impossible. Was he going to kiss her again?

"Hannah? Will you at least think about it?"

Anything, she thought desperately, anything to make him stop looking at her that way, to make him let go of her.

"Yes," she whispered, "all right, I will. I—"

A smile swept across his face. "I knew you'd see it my way," he said triumphantly.

She stared at him in horror. "Grant, no! I only said—"

He drew her into his arms. "I promise you, Hannah, you'll never regret this decision."

SANDRA MARTON is the author of more than thirty romance novels. Readers around the world love her strong, passionate heroes and determined, spirited heroines. When she's not writing, Sandra likes to hike, read, explore out-of-the-way restaurants and travel to faraway places. The mother of two grown sons, Sandra lives with her husband in a sun-filled house in a quiet corner of Connecticut where she alternates between extravagant bouts of gourmet cooking and take-out pizza. Sandra loves to hear from her readers. You can write to her (SASE) at P.O. Box 295, Storrs, Connecticut 06268.

Books by Sandra Marton

HARLEQUIN PRESENTS

1736—A WOMAN ACCUSED
1751—A BRIDE FOR THE TAKING
1780—HOSTAGE OF THE HAWK

LANDON'S LEGACY:
1808—AN INDECENT PROPOSAL
1813—GUARDIAN GROOM
1819—HOLLYWOOD WEDDING
1825—SPRING BRIDE

1860—A PROPER WIFE

SANDRA MARTON

No Need For Love

Harlequin Books

TORONTO • NEW YORK • LONDON
AMSTERDAM • PARIS • SYDNEY • HAMBURG
STOCKHOLM • ATHENS • TOKYO • MILAN
MADRID • WARSAW • BUDAPEST • AUCKLAND

ISBN 0-373-11880-5

NO NEED FOR LOVE

First North American Publication 1997.

This edition published by arrangement with Harlequin Books S.A.

Printed in U.S.A.

CHAPTER ONE

IF THE bit of black satin and lace spilling from the gold foil box wasn't the sexiest nightgown Hannah had ever seen, it was certainly a close contender. It looked as if it might make the man who saw you in it go up in flames the moment you opened its matching peignoir.

'Well?' Sally shifted impatiently from one foot to the other. 'What do you think?'

Hannah poked a finger at the sheer bodice. 'It's—uh—it's very nice.'

'Nice?' Sally made a face. 'It's got to be better than "nice", Hannah. "Nice" is what your mother buys you for sleep-away camp, it's not what the girls you work with give you as a wedding gift!'

Hannah nodded. 'Right. That's what I meant, that it's the perfect present for a bridal shower.' She pushed her oversized glasses up on the bridge of her nose. 'Really.'

'Yeah?' Sally drew the gown towards her, regarded it critically, then let it slip back so it lay draped across the gold box. 'Gosh, I hope so. I've never been the one to choose the gift before. I just hope Betty likes it.'

'I'm sure she will.'

'OK, then, I'm gonna just leave this here until it's time to give it to her—or you can bring it with you when you come to the lunch room, OK?'

'Me? Oh, I can't! I've too much to... do,' Hannah finished lamely as the door swung shut. Sally was gone, leaving only a drift of perfume behind.

Hannah stared at the gown, made a face, and sank down in her chair. Today seemed to be her day for dealing with the two extremes of wedded bliss, she thought. Her forehead creased as she leaned towards her computer and began scrolling through the ugly details of Gibbs vs. Gibbs. What had once been a happy marriage had been reduced to a case file of accusations and rebuttals.

Well, she thought as she began typing, at least there hadn't been any children involved. Her fingers slowed on the keys. That was what people had said about her too, eight long years ago when the pain of her own divorce had been fresh and questions about the future had seemed insurmountable.

'It's a good thing you didn't have kids,' they'd said, and Hannah had agreed. It had been scary enough being responsible for herself, let alone for a baby.

But she'd turned out to be perfectly capable of making a life, a good one, for herself. All it lacked, if it lacked anything, was someone to share it with. Not a man. Never that. But if she'd had a child, a daughter or a son, a smiling face to come home to at the end of the day...

Hannah gave herself a little shake. 'Oh, come on,' she said briskly. Her fingers danced over the computer keyboard. There was no point in wasting time on what might have been. It was now that mattered—and that meant making sense of the Byzantine complications of the case her boss had dumped on to her shoulders just before he'd marched out of the door.

'Do something with this mess,' he'd demanded, dropping several thick files on her desk on his way out.

'Do what?' Hannah had asked, bewildered. She had been Grant MacLean's assistant for five months now, but she'd only helped him with his speciality, international law.

'Make some sense out of it, Miss Lewis,' he'd said, his grey eyes cool. 'You do have some sort of paralegal training, don't you?'

And you're the one who gets paid a fortune to practise law, Hannah had wanted to say. But she hadn't. She liked her job too much to toss it all away. Besides, she'd learned to bite her tongue and let her boss's sharper comments slip by.

Mean MacLean, Sally had dubbed him, and, if it was a cruel nickname, it was close to accurate.

'What a waste,' she'd groaned, 'all that thick black hair, white teeth, rippling muscles, and gorgeous eyes—and a heart so tiny you'd have to perform micro-surgery to find it!'

Hannah sighed as she highlighted a section of text. That wasn't precisely true. Grant MacLean had a heart—rather a busy heart, if his monthly flower and chocolate bill meant anything. It was just that no one who worked for him ever saw it.

It was 'do this,' and 'do that,' with a 'please' added sometimes, a please that never seemed to soften the glacial arrogance in the tone.

Still, there were things that made the job more than palatable. The pay was excellent and, in all truth, MacLean drove himself even harder than he drove her. He was, evidently, a believer in working as hard as he played. And working for him was quite a plum, especially for someone like Hannah who'd been a secretary with a brand new paralegal certificate in her hand only five months ago. He was the firm's shining star, a lawyer with a rapidly developing national and international reputation. Hannah had a sneaking suspicion she hadn't been his first choice for the job, but his last paralegal had quit in a huff one day and, rather than go through the laborious process of interviewing applicants, he'd asked her to work for him.

No. Not asked, exactly. Mr Longworth had recommended her, and Grant MacLean had scowled at her from under his dark brows and said all right, he'd give her a try...

A sudden whoop of laughter echoed down the corridor, dying as a wave of music swept over it. Hannah glanced at her watch. Five o'clock, on the nose. Quitting time at the estimable law firm of Longworth, Hart, Holtz and MacLean, and Betty's party had started. Well, she wasn't going to get there for quite a while, if at all. Gibbs vs. Gibbs was driving her crazy. From what she'd read so far, Jack Gibbs was a sneaky, two-timing rat, but his pathetic wife didn't want to believe it.

Why were women so damned stupid? Why were men such bastards? Why...?

The door banged open. 'Time to get a move on,' Sally called.

Hannah shook her head without looking up. 'I'm nowhere near finished.'

'Oh, come on. It's after five.'

'Exactly. Mr MacLean will be back soon. And he'll expect me to have this brief organised.'

Sally made a face. 'Boy, I'd love to tell him what he can do with his expectations!'

Hannah laughed. 'Wish Betty the best for me, will you?'

'You can do that for yourself. I'll be back in half an hour to pick up this little number.' Sally patted the slinky folds spilling from the gold foil box. 'And when I do, I'm taking you with me!'

Hannah didn't bother protesting as the door slammed shut. She was too busy peering at the screen. For a while, there was no sound in the office except for the soft click of her keyboard and the occasional scratch of her pencil against her notepad. After a long while, she sat back, shoved her glasses atop her head, and rose from her chair.

'Time for a break,' she murmured. She walked the width of her small office, poured herself a cup of coffee, then strolled back again. The black lace nightgown caught her eye; she stopped and caught it up lightly in her hand, shaking her head as she examined the gossamer straps and sheer bodice.

Maybe Betty would be one of the lucky ones and whatever she was dreaming today would last. Maybe her husband would be a man, not the boy Hannah had unwittingly married, who'd been so intent on his own desires that he'd slept with another woman in their bed.

She could still remember the pain of coming home early from work and finding them there, a frill of black lace very like this one on the carpet.

The door swung open and banged against the wall. Sally, Hannah thought, and she swung around blindly and held out the damned nightgown.

'Take this, will you please?' she demanded. 'I don't want it cluttering up my...'

The burst of angry words caught in her throat. She gave a start as she looked into the grey eyes of her employer.

'For me, Miss Lewis?' Grant MacLean took the gown from her suddenly nerveless fingers. It slithered through his hands like a snake. 'Charming,' he said, his voice fairly purring. A little smile angled across his mouth. 'But not quite my size.'

Colour raced into Hannah's cheeks. 'I—I didn't know it was you, Mr MacLean.'

'No. I can see that.' MacLean's gaze drifted impersonally over her, from her neatly clasped chestnut hair to the hazel eyes behind the oversized glasses, then down her grey worsted blazer to the hem of her matching calf-length skirt before returning to her face. He held out the gown as that tight smile inched across his lips again. 'A gift from an admirer, perhaps?'

This time, she felt her face blaze crimson. 'No! Of course not. How could you think...?' She fell silent. He was having fun at her expense, damn him! 'It's a gift,' she said stiffly, snatching the gown from his hands. 'For Betty, in the typing pool. She's getting married Sunday, and——'

MacLean's smile vanished. 'Spare me the details,' he said as he shouldered his way past her. 'Just get your notes on the Gibbs case and come into my office—if you can spare the time, of course.'

Hannah glared at his retreating back. 'Yes, sir.' She gave the nightgown one last, condemning glance, then stuffed it into the box and slammed on the lid. Quickly, she stalked to the door and flung it open. A girl was coming towards her, hurrying towards the employees' lunch room where the sounds of revelry had grown louder. 'Here,' Hannah said, shoving the box into the girl's arms, 'take this.'

'What is it?'

'It's Betty's gi——'

'Miss Lewis!' The voice roared out from behind her and Hannah flinched.

'Just take it,' she hissed, and then she shut the door, snatched up her pad and pencil, and hurried into Grant MacLean's private office.

It was a large room but it was not furnished with the profusion of Oriental carpets and priceless antiques that filled the other partners' quarters. A pair of black leather couches faced a low glass table to her right; to her left, a matching cabinet hid stereophonic equipment and a built-in bar. Ahead, centred against a backdrop of darkened glass, stood a rectangle of burled walnut that served as MacLean's desk, flanked by a pair of leather chairs that complemented the one behind the desk.

It was a room almost spartan in its simplicity, yet it had an air of power and authority almost as tangible as the man it housed. He was standing at the window, his back to Hannah, staring out at the Golden Gate Bridge resplendent in the last rays of the afternoon sun, but one glance at his rigid spine and stiffly held shoulders suggested that he was not admiring the scenery.

Hannah ran her tongue over her lips as she moved towards him. 'Mr MacLean?' She waited for a few seconds. 'Sir? You asked me to bring you my notes on Gibbs.'

'Are you sure you have the time to spare, Miss Lewis?' He swung around to face her. 'Perhaps you'd prefer to attend that fashion show down the hall.'

Her chin lifted. 'That's not necessary, sir, thank you.'

MacLean looked at her in silence, then jerked his head towards the door.

'Close that,' he said sharply. 'My skull already feels as if there's somebody inside hammering to get out without having to listen to the noise coming from that—that female victory party!' Hannah's brows lifted, but she said nothing, only turned and did as he'd asked. Then she marched to his desk, her sensible heels silent against the tightly knit cream Berber carpet. MacLean motioned her to a chair as he loosened his tie and sank into the one behind the desk. 'That stupid woman,' he muttered. 'She wouldn't agree to the settlement.'

Hannah was puzzled, but only for a moment. 'Mrs Gibbs?'

'Yes.' He leaned forward and folded his hands loosely on the desk top. 'We offered one million five, but she won't take it.' He shook his head, the harshly handsome face twisted into lines of disbelief. '"I love him," she keeps saying, as if that were about to change anything. Can you imagine? Of course,' he went on in a smug, certain voice, 'it's all crap.'

He looked at Hannah. It was clear he was waiting for her to say something.

'Is it?'

'Sure. She's just setting him up for the kill. She figures on getting more money out of him. Hell, they were married, what? Five years? What's that worth in dollars?'

Hannah frowned. 'I'm not sure you're right, sir. After reading through the file, I——'

'Well, Gibbs will pay. What choice has he got? But he'll be twice as smart next time. He won't let himself get led into marriage so easily.'

'Mrs Gibbs manoeuvred him into marrying her?'

That smug look came over his face again. 'I keep forgetting that you're single, Miss Lewis. You've no way of knowing that marriage is never a man's idea.'

Hannah's brows lifted. 'Is that right?' she said politely.

'Some pretty little thing comes along, the time is right, and wham, the next thing a man knows, he's being dragged to the altar.'

'Really,' she said, even more politely. 'How remarkable. I saw Mr and Mrs Gibbs the day they came in for that meeting; she seemed rather small to have accomplished such a feat.'

MacLean's head came up sharply. 'It's a figure of speech,' he said.

'Ah.' Hannah bent over her notepad and scratched something on it. 'I should have realised.'

'The point is, the bitch wants blood!'

'Another figure of speech, of course,' she muttered before she could stop herself. She swallowed hard. What was wrong with her? She felt as if the devil were pulling her tongue.

MacLean's eyes narrowed. 'Did you say something, Miss Lewis?'

Hannah took a breath. 'Yes, sir. I said that you're wrong about what Mrs Gibbs wants. She's not after more money. She's still in love with her husband.'

He stared at her for a moment, then shot from his chair. 'When did you speak to her? Damn, she must have gone straight to the telephone after the meeting.' He stalked around the desk, leaned down, and grasped the arms of Hannah's chair. 'What did she say, exactly? I want to know every word.'

Hannah wet her lips. 'She—she didn't.'

'Didn't what?' MacLean's dark brows drew together. 'Surely you can remember.'

'I mean, she didn't telephone.' Did he have to stare down at her like this? He was so close that she could see that his eyes weren't really grey at all; they were a combination of blue and black and green, little streaking lines radiating out from the dark pupil.

'She was here, then?' He shook his head. 'But she couldn't have been. I came straight back; if she'd come by——'

'She didn't do that, either.' Hannah took a deep breath. 'I was—I was just saying what I thought, sir.'

'What?'

'I was—I was only offering my opinion.'

A muted scream of feminine laughter beating through the closed door punctuated her hurried words. Silence fell between them, and then MacLean let out his breath.

'Your opinion,' he said softly. 'Your highly trained opinion as a paralegal, that is.' A muscle knotted in his jaw. 'I see.'

Oh, God, Hannah thought. She forced herself to look directly at him, as if her heart hadn't just plummeted to her feet.

'I thought that's what you...' She swallowed. 'I was reading through the case,' she said, 'as you asked me to do, and——'

'Ah.' He smiled grimly. 'As I asked you to do.'

'Yes, sir. And——'

'Let me try to understand this, Miss Lewis. Did I ask you to formulate an opinion of the case?'

'You asked me to—to do something with it...'

'Yes. Organise the file, perhaps. Write a précis.' He smiled, almost kindly. 'You are familiar with that word, aren't you? You did hear it once or twice when you weren't sleeping through your paralegal courses?'

Hannah's cheeks blazed. 'Mr MacLean, if you'd just let me explain...'

'Perhaps you're a confidante of the delightful Mrs Gibbs?'

'Certainly not.'

'A psychologist, then?'

Her cheeks pinkened. 'I only meant——'

'Or a fortune-teller.' His eyes narrowed. 'Is that what you are, Miss Lewis?'

'Mr MacLean, please——'

'But you know the intricacies of this case.'

'I didn't mean to suggest——'

'Of male-female relationships in general.' His lips drew back from his teeth and he gave her a smile that would have done a shark proud. 'It's wonderful, the things they teach a paralegal nowadays.'

Hannah stiffened. 'It's just common sense, sir. I read the file, and I was simply——'

'Is it your sex that gives you such insight, the fact that you and the lady in question share similar genetic material?' He leaned closer to her and she caught the scent of piney aftershave mingled with sharp male anger. 'Or is it your vast experience in matrimonial law that makes you an expert?'

All at once she shoved back her chair, hard enough so his hands fell away from it, and leaped to her feet.

'You're no expert, either,' she said sharply. 'When I took this job, they said your field was international law. But now—but now...'

The fast, furious words ceased as rapidly as they'd begun. She looked at him in horror. What was she thinking of? She'd been acting crazy ever since she'd stepped into this office. This was Grant MacLean, this was her boss! This was the man whose signature was on her weekly pay cheque, whose orders she was supposed to obey...

'You're right.'

Her mouth dropped open. 'I—I beg your pardon?'

MacLean gave her a tight smile. 'I said, you're right. About my expertise, or my lack of it. I only agreed to take this case because Gibbs is an old friend. I told him at the start to get a divorce lawyer, but he wouldn't hear of it.' He sighed. 'Make a note, please, Miss Lewis. Remind me to telephone him first thing in the morning and tell him I'm resigning from the case. I'll recommend someone else to him.'

An apology, and the word 'please', all in the same breath. Hannah bent her head over her notepad. Just wait until Sally heard about——

'The only thing I really know about marriage is that it's invariably a mistake that people shouldn't make more than once.'

Hannah looked up. He was smiling politely. A peace offering, she thought, and smiled back.

'We're in complete agreement there.'

A little frown of surprise creased his brow. 'Is that the voice of experience talking?'

She hesitated, then nodded. 'I'm afraid it is.'

'And your comment about Mrs Gibbs still loving her husband—was that the voice of experience talking, too?'

Her eyes widened. 'You mean, am I...?' She blew out her breath. 'No,' she said without hesitation, 'it definitely was not.'

Grant MacLean steepled his hands beneath his chin. 'I see.'

Hannah shrugged her shoulders. 'The only thing I'd argue with is how a couple ends up at the altar.'

He nodded. 'Yes?'

'I don't think anyone leads anyone there, I just think they both fool themselves into thinking it's a good idea.'

MacLean chuckled as he leaned back against the desk and folded his arms over his chest.

'And our Mrs Gibbs——'

'—is still fooling herself. Yes, sir. I think so.'

He nodded. 'You think she wants to try and make a go of things, hmm? Very well, then. Make a note of that. I'll tell Gibbs when I talk to him tomorrow.' A moment passed, and then he cleared his throat. 'Please, Miss Lewis, won't you sit down?'

Hannah sat down carefully and crossed her legs at the ankle, notepad and pencil at the ready, all too aware that she had survived a near-disaster. She'd come damnably close to getting herself fired. She'd given away more of herself than she usually did, as well, but that was understandable. Grant MacLean had surprised her with his sudden honesty and self-deprecation; it had elicited an exchange of truth on her part.

Perhaps now they could get on better with each other. Perhaps he wouldn't be quite so sharp-tempered. Hannah looked up, smiling—and the smile froze. MacLean was watching her with an intensity that was almost paralysing, as if—as if she were something pinned to a microscope slide.

'Mr MacLean? Is something wrong?'

He shook his head. 'No, Miss Lewis. Quite the contrary. Everything is fine.'

He didn't look as if everything were fine, Hannah thought. She shifted uncomfortably in her seat, then looked down quickly and opened her notebook.

'I know you said you're going to give up the case,' she said. 'But I did make some notes. Shall I type them up and——?'

'Are you busy this evening, Miss Lewis?'

Hannah blinked. 'Busy?' she said, looking up again. He was still watching her that same way, dammit, as if he were a scientist and she were a new and hitherto unidentified species of bacteria.

'Yes.' He smiled pleasantly. 'Did you have plans, I mean?'

'No, sir. I can work late, if you——'

'Work?' MacLean's smile grew, until it was a grin, the first, she thought suddenly, that she'd ever seen on his face. 'Well, yes, Miss Lewis, I suppose you could call it that.' He leaned back against his desk, crossed his arms over his chest, and looked straight into her eyes. 'You see, I'm in desperate need of your services tonight.'

'Yes, sir. Will you be dictating, or——?'

This time, he laughed aloud. But there was no sharpness to it, only a softness that made the laughter almost a purr, and it made the hair rise on the back of Hannah's neck.

'Miss Lewis. Hannah, I mean. I think, considering the circumstances, I should call you by your given name, don't you?'

Hannah took a deep breath. Something was happening here, something she didn't understand, something—something dangerous.

MacLean leaned away from the desk, then came slowly towards her and held out his hand. She stared at it in silence, then at him, and after a moment he reached out, clasped her fingers in his, and drew her to her feet.

Then he smiled, and Hannah's heart almost stopped beating, for the smile transformed him, turning him with blinding speed from the scourge of Longworth, Hart, Holtz and MacLean into an incredibly sexy male.

'After all, sweetheart,' he said softly, 'only a damned fool would use such formal terms with his mistress.'

CHAPTER TWO

HANNAH stared into the grey eyes a scant few inches from hers. This was a joke, she thought crazily. Her boss was telling a joke with a long delay before the punchline.

But that cocksure grin was still curved across his mouth, and all at once she knew that the only funny thing in this office was her foolishness in having told him that she was a divorced woman. Not that she hadn't been down this road before. Many men thought women like her made easy targets—even, it seemed, a man like Grant MacLean, who had, she was quite certain, never until this moment even noticed that she was female.

Her lip curled in disgust. 'Let go of me,' she demanded.

One dark brow rose in a questioning curve. 'Of course,' he said, his hand falling away from hers.

She clasped the wrist he'd held and rubbed at the skin as if she were trying to eradicate his fingerprints. 'Just who do you think you are?' she said in a low, furious voice.

MacLean stared at her, perplexed, and then, suddenly, he began to smile.

'Miss Lewis—Hannah—I think you've misunderstood me.'

'No. I haven't misunderstood you at all, Mr MacLean. But you've certainly misunderstood me.' Her eyes met his. 'I am not the least bit interested in your—your proposition.'

His smile broadened. 'Let me explain before you——'

'You're wasting your time.'

'I don't think so, Hannah.'

'Believe me, you are.' She stared at him a second longer, then turned and marched stiffly to the door. 'If that's all, *sir*,' she said, flinging the word like an insult over her shoulder, 'I'll go back to my office and finish my work on the ——'

'Hannah, dammit, wait a minute!'

'—the Gibbs case.' Her hand closed on the doorknob and she yanked it open. 'I'll print out my notes and leave them on your desk before——'

He came up behind her with an amazing swiftness for a man of his size, and the knob was wrenched from her hand as he slammed the door shut.

'Open that door,' she said. Her voice shook a little, not so much with fear as with righteous indignation. How dared he? How *dared* he? 'Dammit, Mr MacLean——'

'You're being a fool, Miss Lewis.'

The humour had fled his voice. His tone was sharp, his grasp unyielding as he caught her by the shoulders and hauled her around to face him. Hannah met his cold gaze with one of her own.

'Stop now,' she said quietly, 'and I'll forget this ever happened.'

MacLean's eyes narrowed. 'Didn't anyone ever teach you that it can be dangerous to make threats?'

'Or do you prefer that I report you?'

'Listen here, young woman——'

'No, sir, *you* listen here. I am not interested in—in fun and games, do you understand? I'm not interested in destroying your career, either, but if you persist in . . .' Her words faded to silence. He was smiling again. Smiling, damn him! 'I assure you,' she said through her teeth, 'there's nothing funny about this.'

'Fantastic,' he said softly. 'Five months of "Yes, Mr MacLean, no, Mr Maclean," five months and never another word out of you, and now here you are, threatening to bring the roof down on my head.'

'And I will, if you don't——'

'I am *not* trying to seduce you.'

Colour stole into Hannah's cheeks. 'I can hardly disagree with that,' she said. 'Seduction is supposed to be subtle, but this approach of yours is——'

'Thank you for the clarification, Miss Lewis. I'm sure it will prove useful in my relationships with women. Now, if you'd just pay attention to me for a minute——'

'I'll count to three,' she said, folding her arms over her breasts, 'and then——'

'Shall I put it more bluntly?'

'You've been blunt enough. If I were you——'

'If you were me,' he said, his tone frigid, 'you would know that you are the last woman on earth I'd ask to be my mistress, Miss Lewis.'

'One. Two. Th...' Suddenly, his words penetrated. She stared at him. 'What?'

His smile vanished; his brows drew together in a harsh frown. 'You're my assistant, for God's sake. You're not a woman.'

The breath puffed from Hannah's lungs. 'Oh,' she said, her voice small and puzzled.

MacLean nodded. 'All I'm interested in,' he said, stroking his finger across his chin, 'is a bit of harmless deception.'

She shook her head in confusion. 'I—I don't understand.'

He turned and strode across the room. When he reached the windows, he rocked back on his heels, stuffed his hands into his trouser pockets, and paid rapt attention to the view.

'I've a party to attend this evening.'

'Yes, I know. The reception for the principals in the Hungarian deal. I noted it on your calendar myself.'

'An hour of ridiculous chit-chat,' he said coldly, 'fuelled by pricey champagne that flows like water and enough canapés to feed an army, then a five-course meal catered by Julia Childs' latest guru, all interspersed with a dozen turns around the dance-floor...'

Hannah couldn't help but smile. 'How terrible for you.'

MacLean swung towards her. His scowl had deepened so that there were two harsh curves rimming his mouth. 'I'm sure my distress stirs your heart, Miss Lewis. But I assure you, it will be a horrible few hours. Oh, I can survive the food and the drinks, I suppose, and the dance band. But an evening of Magda Karolyi...' A shudder went through him. 'God, that's more than any man should have to bear!'

'Magda Karolyi?' It sounded like an exotic dessert, but from the look on her boss's face it was bound to be more than that.

'The sister of the head of the Hungarian group. We met in Budapest last year, when I was there putting this deal together.'

'Mr MacLean.' Hannah cleared her throat. 'This is all very interesting, sir. But——'

'She's a very attractive woman.' A slow wave of colour beat up under the tanned skin that lay across his high cheekbones. 'And she's—she's taken an interest in me.'

Hannah stared at him. 'She's taken an...?'

'Dammit,' he snarled, 'must I spell it out? The bloody woman did everything but crawl into my bed in Budapest. Avoiding her was like walking a tightrope; I only got away with it because I kept claiming I was too busy with meetings and planning sessions to—to accommodate.' His eyes flashed to Hannah's, the coldness in them daring her to so much as smile, but she was far too amazed that he should reveal all this about himself to react with anything but rapt attention. 'She's the apple of her brother's eye.'

'The brother who's in charge of——'

'Yes.' MacLean blew out his breath. 'If she's not happy, he's not happy.'

'Are you saying that—that he'll expect you to—to...?'

'No, of course not! He won't "expect" me to do anything—except be nice to her. Pleasant. Gracious.' His mouth twisted. 'All the things one human being generally tries to be to another.'

Hannah held out her hands. 'Well, then, I don't see...'

'The trouble is that Magda is sure to misinterpret everything and anything—including the fact that I'm going to show up at this damned party without a woman on my arm.'

'Then why will you? I mean, why didn't you ask someone to go with you?'

'Dammit, Miss Lewis, what do you take me for? I'm not a fool!' He turned and paced from one end of the pale Berber carpet to the other, spine ramrod-straight, shoulders taut. 'I had a date for this evening. But—but the lady and I have decided not to see each other for a while.' Hannah said nothing, and the colour in his face darkened. 'Our relationship had become—complicated.'

'Like the Magda Karolyi thing?' she said, staring at him.

'No! Not at all.' His glare was formidable. 'Why is it women who start out claiming they are not interested in permanency so often are?'

'Ah.' Hannah nodded. 'I see.'

'The point is,' he said coldly, 'it's left me in an awkward position. I have no choice but to attend this evening's function, but I've no wish to do it alone.' There was a dramatic pause. 'And that's where you come in.'

She stared at him. You arrogant bastard, she thought...

'You want me to go to this party with you.'

'Exactly.'

'And pretend that we're—involved.'

'Yes.'

Hannah gave a sharp little laugh. 'I'm sorry, Mr MacLean, but it's out of the question.'

'Why?' The black scowl darkened his face again. 'Why is it out of the question?'

'What do you mean, why? It—it just is.'

'That's not a reason, that's a statement.'

'I should think it's obvious,' she said. 'Deception like that——'

'I'd be the one doing the lying, not you. All you'd have to do is smile and say hello, drink some champagne and eat some of that damned stuff they call food at these overblown bashes. What's so difficult about that?'

Hannah stared at him. How could he ask her such a question? And why should she want to make a fool of some woman she'd never even met? He made it sound as if he'd been an innocent in all this, but that didn't mean anything.

'What's the problem, Miss Lewis? Don't you believe me? I tell you, the woman's trouble with a short fuse.'

And she was interested in Grant MacLean. That Hannah could believe. He was a good-looking man, she had to give him that. If you weren't working for him, enduring his demands and his drive for perfection, he was probably a rather interesting male—if you liked the type.

'Well?' His voice was sharp. 'What do you say?'

She looked up. She had already said it, but it was clear that he had no intention of listening to any answer but the one he wanted. He was watching her through narrowed eyes, arms folded across his chest, mouth set in a taut, narrow line. It was a sight she'd seen before, during meetings with important clients and their sometimes intractable opponents. The authoritative tone, the determined posture, even the cool, never-wavering set of those glacial grey eyes, all worked together to achieve his goal.

But Hannah wasn't about to be intimidated. She had absolutely no intention of being part of his little game. If he was really having a problem with Magda Karolyi, it was up to him to get out of it on his own.

'The party's at the Mark Hopkins. Have you ever been there?'

Hannah shook her head. 'No, no, I haven't.'

'It's a handsome place, Hannah. You'll like it.'

'Oh, I'm sure I will. I mean, I'm sure I would, if——'

'I'll send you home by taxi, when the evening ends.'

'Mr MacLean, there's really no point in——'

'If it's the idea of pretending we're intimate that bothers you——'

'It isn't that.' Their eyes met, and colour flooded her cheeks. 'Well, it is, but that's only part of——'

'Magda needn't think we're lovers, I suppose. It will be enough that I'm with another woman.'

But she wasn't a woman. Hadn't he just said so? She was his assistant.

'I really don't see the problem here. Unless—have you another engagement tonight?'

She looked at him blankly. 'No,' she admitted. 'I just don't think...I mean, this isn't—it's not part of my job, after all.'

'Would it make you feel better if it were? Then think of it that way—as part of your job description. When you signed on for this position, I made it clear that this wasn't a job for someone with a nine-to-five mentality. You said you understood. In fact, you gave me your assurance that you would give me your very best at all times. Do you remember?'

Hannah flushed. 'Of course. But I never meant—I never thought *you* meant——'

'Haven't you ever attended a social event as part of your job, Miss Lewis?'

'Yes, once or twice. But those times were different. They were receptions given by the firm for——'

'This is the same thing.'

'It isn't,' she said firmly. 'Longworth, Hart, Holtz and MacLean aren't hosting this. And you've no right to——'

'A matter of semantics,' he said, shrugging away her comment as if he were brushing off a fly. 'The evening is simply part of your workload. Have I mentioned that you'll be on overtime?'

'That's very generous of you, sir. But——'

His brows drew together. 'Look, Miss Lewis, I can't spend the next hour debating this. Can you work late tonight or can't you?'

Hannah stared at him. 'Work late tonight? Well, yes, if you——'

'Good girl.' He reached past her and opened the door to the outer office. 'Be ready to leave in fifteen minutes.' His hand brushed lightly across her hair, then touched her cheek and, for reasons that made no sense whatsoever, a feeling of lightness engulfed her. 'And do something with yourself, please,' he said, not unkindly. 'Let your hair loose, put on some lipstick—we're going to a party, not a conference. All right?'

No, Hannah thought, it was not all right at all, but how could she tell him that, when she was already standing on the other side of the closed door?

Fifteen minutes later, he came striding out of his office. 'Ready?' he asked crisply.

Hannah turned. 'Yes,' she said, giving the single word as much irritation, annoyance and downright anger as she could manage. But MacLean didn't seem to notice. Instead, he marched towards her, clasped her by the shoulders, and drew her under the uncompromising glare of an overhead fluorescent lamp.

'The lipstick's fine. A little pale, but it complements your colouring.' He frowned. 'I don't suppose you have another blouse on hand?'

Her chin lifted. 'No,' she said tightly, 'I do not.'

'Well, this will have to do.' He reached out and closed his fingers around the top button. Hannah caught his wrist, but he brushed her hand aside. 'You look like a schoolgirl, Miss Lewis. Surely you don't go out on dates wearing blouses closed to the collar, do you?'

'This is not a date,' she said stiffly. 'And I really resent...'

Two buttons slipped out of their holes; she felt the swift, impersonal brush of his fingertips against her skin, and that strange, out-of-body feeling went through her again.

'That's better.' His gaze moved over her slowly. 'A little informal, perhaps, but not unacceptable.' A frown creased his forehead. 'I thought I told you to wear your hair loose.'

Her hand went to her hair, drawn back, as usual, neatly on her neck and held in a tortoiseshell clip.

'I always wear it this way,' she said defensively.

'Yes. I've noticed.' The clip came loose, and her hair tumbled free. 'But you're going to wear it differently tonight,' he said, as he thrust his hands into her hair and drew it over her shoulders. When he was done, he held her at arm's length and inspected her with slow, almost insulting care. Hannah's chin tilted.

'Will I do?' she asked in a frigid voice.

His gaze moved to her face, drifted across her features, and then that little angular smile tilted across his mouth.

'Yes,' he said, and he sounded almost as surprised as she felt when the softly spoken word sent a little rush of pleasure tingling through her blood.

Well, she thought quickly, why wouldn't it? A compliment from Mean MacLean was as rare as a blizzard in July. Naturally she'd react to such a thing.

They taxied to the hotel in silence, he sitting against the window on the right side, frowning over scrawled notes in a pocket diary, Hannah on the left. She was grateful he wasn't attempting any small talk; she was still angry at how she'd been bulldozed into playing a part in a charade to dupe an innocent woman. She glanced at her watch. It was just past six-thirty. If these things went as they usually did, she'd be safely back in a cab again by ten o'clock. Nine-thirty, if she was lucky.

She looked at Grant MacLean again. He'd been a trial lawyer with a reputation for never losing before he'd taken up his esoteric speciality in international law, and it was easy to see how he'd got that reputation. Once he'd determined what he wanted of her, he'd never backed down. He'd been willing to do whatever it took: he'd bullied, threatened, cajoled, dangled rewards—anything to get his own way. Her gaze moved over him, taking in the slightly jutting nose, the firm jaw, the powerful body contained within the carefully tailored navy wool suit. He was a formidable opponent; it would be frightening to go head to head with him over something that really mattered.

He was, as well, an awfully attractive man. Sally and the other girls always said so, but Hannah had never paid his looks very much attention. For one thing, she'd learned her lesson years ago about good looks: a handsome face and hard body were just superficial trappings. It was the inner man that counted.

For another—she shifted in her seat. For another, she'd never really looked at him as a man, until tonight. He'd always just been her boss, Mr MacLean, until five minutes ago, when he'd handed her into the cab.

'Thank you, sir,' she'd said stiffly, and he'd given her a look cold enough to freeze water.

'Be sure and address me that way in front of Miss Karolyi,' he'd said, his voice heavy with sarcasm. 'That's bound to convince her you're my date.'

Grant. She was to call him Grant. Grant...

'We're here.'

Hannah looked up. The cab had pulled to the kerb; a uniformed doorman was holding the door open and smiling politely at her. She stepped on to the pavement and gazed at the hotel. A laughing couple were strolling up the steps to the main door, she in a gauzy cocktail gown, he in a dark suit, their arms wrapped tightly around each other's waists, and suddenly she wondered why in heaven's name she'd let herself be talked into this. She wasn't dressed right, for one thing, and she could never carry it off. She didn't *want* to carry it off. Grant MacLean was her employer, he controlled her nine-to-five life, and hadn't he said he didn't see her as a woman?

'Are you all right?' His voice was low, his breath warm against her ear. Hannah looked at him as his fingers closed lightly around her arm.

'This isn't going to work,' she said in a quick rush, and he gave her that smile he'd given her a lifetime ago, when he'd first asked her to take part in this game.

'Of course it will, sweetheart,' he whispered, and then, before she could draw back, he cupped her face in his hand, bent to her, and put his mouth to hers. The kiss was brief, the press of his lips firm and cool, but when he drew back her heart was racing as if it wanted to escape her breast.

'Don't,' she spat. 'You have no right——'

She caught her breath as he kissed her again, his mouth closing over hers with gentle persuasion. She felt the light brush of his tongue against her lips, then its warm thrust. A tremor went through her, not of revulsion or even anger but of something far more primitive and powerful.

Grant drew back. A smile of satisfaction curved across his lips.

'Yes,' he said softly, 'that's much better.'

'You—you——'

'Magda's not a fool, Hannah. Telling her we're intimate won't serve any purpose if you don't look the part.'

'Intimate?' she stuttered. 'Are you crazy? We agreed I'd be your date; you said——'

'But you look convincing now, with that little flush on your cheeks and that swollen softness to your mouth.' He took her hand and tucked it into the crook of his arm. 'Now smile, sweetheart, and look at me as if you've just come from my bed.'

'You can't do this to me,' she said as he hurried her along beside him—but he was already propelling her up the steps and through the door. By the time they reached the ballroom they'd been stopped by half a dozen people.

Hannah ached to turn her back and walk away from him, to leave him on his own and let him fend off all the predatory women in Hungary with his own devices. But how could she storm away from the president of the Chamber of Commerce in the middle of an introduction, or the director of the San Francisco Symphony? How could she ignore the head of the largest bank on the West Coast, or the mayor? And then there was the one person no one could ignore, a woman in a crimson gown that looked as if it had been spray-painted on, all creamy shoulders, breathtaking décolletage, and masses of golden curls piled high atop her head. She came bearing down on them with a little shriek of delight, and Hannah knew immediately who she was.

'Magda Karolyi?' she whispered.

Grant tensed beside her. 'Yes,' he muttered, 'dear God, that's her!'

'Grant,' the blonde said, launching herself at him, 'oh, darling, how vunderful to zee you again!'

He twisted his head at the last second, so that her kiss fell on his cheek and not his mouth. Then he stepped back, put his arm around Hannah's waist, and drew her forward.

'Magda,' he said pleasantly, 'it's wonderful to see you, too.'

The blonde's eyes, a dark chocolate that contrasted vividly with her pale hair, gave Hannah a quick, assessing glance.

'This is Hannah Lewis, Magda. Hannah, you remember all the things I told you about Magda, don't you?' He looked down at her, his eyes filled with warning.

Hannah gave him a long, steady look. You put your life in my hands, Grant MacLean, she thought, and now you're going to get what you deserve. She smiled, took a deep breath, and turned to Magda Karolyi.

'Miss Karolyi,' she said, 'Mr MacLean asked me here tonight, and now I feel I owe you an apology.'

Her voice faded away, but not because of the sudden pressure of Grant's hand on her waist. It was Magda who was responsible. Hannah stiffened as the chocolate-coloured eyes swept across her. She could feel the other woman taking inventory, dismissing the plain silk blouse, the grey blazer and skirt as beneath contempt, moving upwards to Hannah's face, noting the simple fall of shining hair, the minimum of make-up, even the lack of jewellery.

A little smile settled on to the pouting crimson lips, and Magda Karolyi turned her back to Hannah in complete, unsubtle dismissal.

'You naughty boy, Grant,' she purred, 'vy haven't you telephoned? I've been in San Francisco two whole days, vaiting for your call.'

Hannah touched the tip of her tongue to her lips. 'That's what I was about to explain, Miss Karolyi.' The blonde turned towards her with a look of sharp irritation. Hannah smiled and moved more closely into the curve of Grant's arm. 'It's my fault Grant hasn't called you.' She gave him a sidelong glance from under her lashes. He was watching her closely, his face expressionless. 'I'm his assistant, you see, and we've been so terribly involved. At the office, I mean. We never seem to find the time...' She tilted her head so that her hair swung softly back from her face. 'Isn't that right, Grant?'

There was a moment of silence, and then Grant cleared his throat.

'Hannah's my paralegal, Magda.'

'Yes,' the blonde said coldly, 'I'm sure she is.'

'She does all the groundwork for the cases I handle. I—uh—I don't know what I'd do without her.'

Magda Karolyi gave him a sharp look. 'Is that so?'

Hannah leaned her head against Grant's shoulder. 'Well, I certainly try my best,' she said sweetly.

Magda's mouth narrowed into a tight line. 'I bet you do,' she said coldly. 'It's been good zeeing you again, Grant. Now, if you'll excuse me, I see some other guests I must greet.' Her eyes shifted to Hannah. 'Miss Lewis.'

'Miss Karolyi.' Hannah smiled cheerfully. 'It's been—delightful.'

The woman's nostrils flared. 'Indeed,' she said, then turned on her heel and stalked away. There was another silence, and then Grant began to laugh softly.

'Well,' he said, 'that takes care of Magda.'

Hannah drew away from him. 'I hope so.'

'Damn, but I wish I could have recorded that. I thought you were going to feed me to the sharks and instead you put a knife right into Magda's—' he grinned '—heart.'

'Her padded heart,' she said coldly. 'And I certainly didn't do it for you.'

His smile faded as he looked at her. 'No,' he said, 'I didn't think you had.'

Hannah took a deep breath. 'Don't make the mistake of thinking you can try this little trick again. I'll endure the rest of the evening because I said that I would, but when it ends, so does your right ever again to drag me into a scheme like this.'

A slow smile curved across Grant MacLean's mouth. 'Threats again, Miss Lewis?'

'Statement, Mr MacLean. I don't like being intimidated.'

'And I,' he said quietly, 'don't like being spoken to as if I were a schoolyard bully.'

Hannah looked at him. He was still smiling; she knew that to anyone in the crowded room it would look as if he was saying something pleasant, even intimate. But his eyes had gone dark and cool; there was a glint in their depths that sent a faint chill up her spine and she wished there were some way to back off without it looking as if she was backing down.

But there was none, and so she stood her ground and met those cold eyes.

'Then don't act like one,' she said softly.

She heard the quick intake of his breath, saw the sudden way his mouth twisted—but then it was over, gone so quickly it might not have happened.

'Grant,' a deep male voice said happily, and within seconds they were enclosed in a group of laughing guests. There was a lot of hand-shaking and back-slapping.

'This is Hannah Lewis," Grant said. His eyes met hers, and he gave her a little smile. 'She insists that I introduce her as my legal assistant. Isn't that right, Hannah?''

It was the sort of remark that made everyone laugh. It was also the sort of remark that intimated she was anything *but* his legal assistant. Still, he treated her with courtesy and propriety, enough so that she was convinced that she had got through the worst of the evening.

A little after nine, just as the tables were being cleared and the dance band was settling in, Grant made apologies for their early departure, drew back Hannah's chair, and led her out of the hotel.

'Aren't we staying for the dancing?' she said, before she could think. 'I mean, won't your friends think it strange that you left early?'

Grant barely glanced at her as he handed her into a taxi and climbed in after her.

'It was a business evening, Miss Lewis, not a social one. I thought I explained that earlier.'

His voice was cold. Hannah risked a quick look at him as the cab pulled out from the kerb.

'I only meant——'

'Where do you live?'

She told him her address and he leaned forward and repeated it to the driver. Then he settled into the far corner of the seat, folded his arms across his chest, and clamped his lips together.

By the time they reached the three-storey town house in which her flat was located, an oppressive silence had settled between them. Hannah threw open the door and scrambled on to the pavement.

'Goodnight,' she said quickly, 'I'll see you in the——' The door slammed shut behind her and a steely hand clamped around her arm. 'What are you doing?' she demanded. It was a stupid question. What he was doing was marching her swiftly to the house, then up the steps.

'Your keys,' he said sharply.

'You don't have to see me in,' she said with sudden wariness.

'Your keys, Miss Lewis.'

The frost in his voice made all the difference. It was clear he was not intent on anything but seeing her safely inside. Leaving a woman alone on the street at night, even at this hour and in this relatively quiet neighbourhood, was, apparently, not something Grant MacLean did—probably, she thought uncharitably, because he was afraid of the possible legal ramifications.

She snapped open her purse and dug out the keys. 'Here,' she said, just as coldly. The door swung open and she held out her hand. He ignored it.

'What floor are you on?'

'The third. But——'

He took her arm and ushered her to the curving staircase that led up into shadowy darkness. They climbed in silence; when they reached the top floor, Hannah was not foolish enough to try and send him on his way. He was going to see her to her door, that was obvious, and trying to stop him again would only let him emphasise which of them was in control.

So far, she seemed to be losing.

When they reached her door, she stopped and faced him.

'My keys, please.' He held them out, his smile as polite as hers. The keys dropped into her open palm. 'Thank you,' she said. 'Goodnight, Mr MacLean.'

'Miss Lewis?'

She had just inserted her key in the lock when he spoke. What now? she thought irritably, and swung around to face him.

'Mr MacLean,' she said wearily, 'it's getting late. And—— '

The words caught in her throat. He was smiling, but it was the kind of smile that made her wish desperately that she could flee inside and slam the door between them.

'You're a hell of a good legal assistant. But you're a phoney when it comes to being a woman.'

She gasped, but it was too late. His arms went around her, he pushed her against the door, and his mouth came down hard on hers.

He had kissed her twice on this night, but not like this. No man should kiss a woman like this, Hannah thought desperately as she slammed her hands against his chest. This wasn't a kiss, it was an exercise in control, brute masculine control, passionless and degrading. She whimpered and tried to twist her face from his, but it was impossible.

A shudder went through her, more of abhorrence at this invasion of her senses than of fear. It was as if he'd been waiting for that signal. He drew back instantly. When he spoke, his tone was frigid.

'I just wanted to be certain there was no mistake about the language. You called me a bully earlier tonight, Hannah. Well, that's the way a bully would behave.'

'And what did you expect me to call you?' Her voice shook as she wiped the back of her hand across her mouth. 'My date? My lover?'

'Ah, Hannah, Hannah.' He laughed. 'If I *were* your lover, I'd kiss you goodnight properly.' Before she could stop him, he plucked the glasses from her nose. 'Like this,' he whispered, and drew her to him.

His mouth caught hers with almost lazy insolence. Hannah tried to pull back, but he clasped her face in his hands and went on kissing her, slowly, gently, his mouth moving on hers, his thumbs stroking across her cheekbones—and suddenly, with no warning at all, she felt warmth flood through her body.

The hands that had been pushing against his chest curled into the lapels of his jacket instead. A muted sound of male triumph growled from his throat and he caught her tightly to him, holding her and kissing her until the world had no meaning...

And then he put her from him. Hannah swayed unsteadily on her feet, stunned, trying to make sense out of what had happened. Their eyes met. For a heartbeat she thought he was as confused as she, but then he slipped the glasses back on her nose and she knew it hadn't been confusion she'd seen at all but smug, patronising satisfaction.

'Thank you for an interesting evening, Hannah.' He started for the stairs, then turned back at the last moment. 'Oh, by the way, it's all right if you want to come in late tomorrow.' He laughed softly. 'Hell, after the hard work you've put in, you're entitled to a good night's sleep.'

And then he was gone.

CHAPTER THREE

HANNAH slipped into a black wool coat-dress, buttoned it, then strode to the mirror and looked at her reflection. Yes. It was perfect. The dress had been an extravagance, costly not because of its classic style but because of the perfection of its fabric and workmanship, bought on sale in a moment of weakness but never yet worn. She'd saved it for a special occasion—but who would have dreamed that that would be the day she left her job?

Because that was what she would be doing today, she thought grimly as she slipped on black leather pumps. What choice did she have? There wasn't a way in the world she could to go on working for Grant MacLean. She'd decided that within the first five minutes after he'd left last night.

What had taken a little longer was determining exactly how to quit. Her first instinct had been to just not show up in the morning, let him come to work and find himself without an assistant.

But that would have been a mistake. She was entitled to a decent reference after four years at Longworth, Hart, Holtz and MacLean. More than that, she'd be damned if she didn't make her reasons for quitting absolutely clear. Otherwise, MacLean would make up a bunch of lies that would salve his monumental ego and leave her looking like a fool.

Hannah stared into the mirror. 'I am resigning,' she said in a clear voice, 'because you, Mr MacLean, are an overbearing, arrogant male chauvinist. And—if they weren't among the nicer creatures—I'd say "pig," too.'

He was the kind of man who should wear animal skins instead of Savile Row suits, and to continue in his employ would be sentencing herself to purgatory. Of course,

Grant MacLean would not see himself that way. God's gift to women, that was what he thought he was. Just look at the elaborate plot he'd hatched to evade Magda Karolyi.

Hannah grimaced as she brushed her hair back from her face. And it wasn't terribly difficult to imagine the scene that must have taken place between him and the woman she'd replaced last night when that nameless fool had begun to expect a more permanent relationship with him.

The man wasn't any sort of gift as far as she was concerned, Hannah thought as she clipped her hair into place at the nape of her neck. The question wasn't how many women Grant MacLean had made fools of in the past, it was whether any of them had told him what a bastard he was.

She, however, would. She'd face him in his lair and tell him what she thought of him, because, if she didn't, he was certain to think he'd triumphed last night when he'd forced his kisses on her. Hell, he'd probably tell himself she was ashamed to face him.

Hannah glared at the mirror. 'You'd love to think that, Mr MacLean, wouldn't you?' she said.

Yes. She just bet he would. It would do a lot more for his overblown ego if he believed she'd clung to him, when in truth the stress of the evening had suddenly caught up to her and taken its toll.

'It was vertigo, Mr MacLean,' she said coldly to the mirror. 'What else did you think it was?'

That he'd forced her into participating in an ugly scheme was bad enough, but then he'd made things even worse by trying to humble her, and all because she'd dared tell him what someone should have told him years ago: that he was a bully and that he couldn't get away with such behaviour in today's world.

Hannah glanced into the mirror one last time and permitted herself a faint smile of satisfaction. She looked cool and controlled, the very epitome of a professional.

'You're not a woman, Miss Lewis,' MacLean had said yesterday, 'you're my assistant.'

That was exactly right, and why his words should have given her even a moment's pause was beyond her. She *was* a professional, not a toy to be played with.

She drew a deep breath, picked up her handbag, and marched to the door. If her divorce had taught her anything, it was that she was a capable human being, one who could take charge of her own life. She didn't have to stay in this job and be humiliated. She would find another job, as good or better. But first, she would make absolutely certain that Grant MacLean knew she had his number—and that his conservative, very proper colleagues, Longworth, Hart and Holtz, knew it, too.

The thought brought the first real smile of the day to her lips.

Hannah had timed things so she'd be sure to arrive long before her employer did. That was why finding a stack of file folders beside her computer and a terse note instructing her to deal with them immediately was a bit disconcerting.

'Miss Lewis,' it read. 'Extract all appropriate references to the French incorporation and have them on my desk by ten.' It was sighed, as always, with the single name, 'MacLean.'

It was the sort of note he left her all the time, so commonplace that she almost began doing as directed. But then she stopped, folder in hand. She looked up quickly, half expecting to see him watching her from the doorway with, no doubt, a smug little smile on his face.

But he wasn't there. How could he be? She'd marched into his office and checked the minute she'd arrived, just to make sure. Still, she made a show of slapping down the folder, picking up the note, and ripping it to bits. Smiling disdainfully, she dropped the shredded paper into the wastebasket.

'Take care of it yourself, MacLean,' she said coolly.

Then she turned on her computer, stabbed her glasses on to her nose, and set to work.

Twenty minutes later, the laser printer spewed out a brief but pointed letter of resignation. Hannah was very pleased with it. It was concise and to the point, outlining what had happened last evening in crisp, no-nonsense terms. She would put a copy of it on the desk of each member of the firm before she went out of the door—which she would do in record time, for she had no intention whatsoever of giving Mr Grant MacLean more than an hour's notice.

She almost laughed when she thought of the note he'd left her. Let him extract his 'appropriate references' while he tried to explain her charges to Longworth, Hart and Holtz. Grant MacLean, eminent lawyer, was about to become Grant MacLean, tightrope walker. And if he lost his balance and fell, thanks to her, it was exactly what he deserved.

'I take it you've gotten the information I require.'

The cool male voice made her jump. Hannah spun around, hand to her throat. MacLean was lounging in the doorway to her office, arms folded across his chest, a dark scowl on his face.

'Mr MacLean!' *Mr* MacLean? she thought, hearing herself. And said in a squeaky voice, too. Damn! That was hardly a good way to start.

'Who did you expect?'

'But—where did you come from?' she said, much more calmly. 'I checked your office...'

'I was in the washroom.'

Of course! He had a private lavatory; all the partners did. And he'd either tossed water on his face or showered—she could see little droplets glistening in his hair. He hadn't shaved yet—there was a rough stubble on his face, just as there'd been last night when he'd kissed her. But the stubble didn't feel rough at all. It had felt silken against her skin, silken and——

'Should I have left you a note to that effect?'

She blinked. He was glaring at her, his mouth set and stern. A flush rose and arced across her cheeks.

'No,' she said quickly, 'No, of course not. I just—you startled me, that's all.'

What was she doing? First her thoughts had drifted in a way that made no sense whatsoever, and now she was stumbling all over herself in what sounded, even to her, like an apology.

She drew herself up, her fingers clutching her notice of resignation even more tightly. All right. He'd caught her off guard. He was good at that. But that was no reason to retreat. It was important that she take the offensive here, that she be the one to——

'I asked you a question, Hannah.'

She stared at him. Her mind was blank.

'What question?'

His mouth twisted. 'Have you found the information I requested?' His gaze went to the file folders stacked on her desk. 'I can see for myself that you haven't.'

Her glance followed his. 'Well, no. I haven't. But——'

'I'll need that information by one o'clock. I've an important meeting this evening, and I'll want time to incorporate what you find into my notes.'

'Yes, sir. I...'

Hannah clamped her lips together. Yes, sir? *Yes, sir*? She took a deep breath.

'What I mean is, yes, I understand. But——'

'Good.' He peered at his wristwatch, then swung on his heel and stepped back into his office. 'Bring me what I need as soon as you have it. Until then, I don't want to be disturbed.'

'Wait a second——'

The door slammed shut. She stood staring at it for a moment, and then she uttered a short, succinct word, marched towards it, and yanked it open.

'Mr MacLean.'

He looked up from his desk. 'Hannah,' he said irritably, 'when I said I didn't want to be disturbed, I meant it.'

'Mr MacLean,' she repeated, 'about those files——'

'Is there a problem?'

Is there a problem? She wanted to laugh in his face. Instead, she nodded and gave him a cool smile.

'Yes. There certainly is.'

'I know they're not very well organised.' He frowned, capped his pen, and leaned forward, clasping his hands on his desk blotter. 'My former assistant was in charge of such things, and I'm afraid *she* wasn't very well organised.'

'That's not the point, Mr MacLean. The files aren't——'

'But then, I'm sure you've already figured that out for yourself, haven't you?'

Hannah looked at him. 'Figured what out for myself?' she asked helplessly.

'That Mrs LaMott wasn't the most qualified of paralegals.' He sighed deeply and rubbed his hands over his face. 'Hell, I'm sorry I'm such a bear this morning.' He gave her a quick, easy smile, the sort she'd seen fewer than half a dozen times in almost as many months. 'I guess I'm not at my best before my first cup of coffee.'

Was that a reminder that she hadn't put up the usual pot? Hannah's expression grew cool.

'How unfortunate.'

MacLean nodded. 'You're right. It's a bad habit—one Mrs LaMott almost broke me of by making the worst cup of coffee this side of China. Nothing like the coffee you brew.' He smiled again. 'Nor was she ever as capable or efficient as you are.'

Hannah stared at him. Did he really think he could gloss over what he'd done last night by patting her on the head as if she were a child? Next he'd be offering her a bribe to forget it all, only he wouldn't call it a bribe, naturally, he'd call it a raise or a bonus——

He frowned. 'I don't suppose you've made coffee just yet?'

'No,' Hannah said coldly, 'I did not, and I've no intention of making any. In fact——'

'That's all right.' He rose from his chair and strolled to the built-in bar across the room. 'I drink too much of the stuff as it is,' he said, opening the concealed miniature refrigerator and taking out a small bottle of chilled mineral water. He poured a glass, then looked at her, brows elevated. 'Would you like some?'

'No,' she said coldly, but somehow the words 'thank you' slipped out, as well. All right, she thought, enough of this. He had managed to defeat her every thrust with a parry, but that was over now. She cleared her throat and took a step forward. 'Mr MacLean.'

'Grant,' he said, quite pleasantly. 'I should think that would be appropriate, after last night, wouldn't you?'

So. They were about to get down to the nitty-gritty.

Hannah's head lifted. 'That's precisely what I want to talk about,' she said grimly. 'Last night.'

'Yes.' He put down the glass and walked back to his desk. 'About last night,' he said as he sank into his chair. 'I want to thank you for your co-operation.'

Whatever she'd expected him to say, it wasn't that. Hannah frowned. 'Thank me?'

'Of course. After all, I dragged you out of here at the very last minute, without so much as a by-your-leave.' He smiled, and she thought crazily that perhaps she ought to be writing down the frequency of those smiles. 'You weren't just being polite when you assured me you had no prior engagement, were you?'

'No,' she said automatically.

'Good, good. I thought about that on my way to work this morning, you know. After all, an employee as diligent and dedicated as you might well put her own needs after the needs of the firm.'

Her eyes flashed to his face. Was he being sarcastic? If he was, she couldn't see any signs. He looked—he looked the way old Mr Longworth looked at the

Christmas party each year, when he gave gold watches to the employees that were retiring. He looked serious and forthright. He looked—he looked sincere.

'Your assistance was invaluable.'

She swallowed. 'It was?'

He nodded. 'Not only did you help me avoid Magda Karolyi, but you also did quite a job of spreading goodwill for the firm.'

Don't answer, she told herself, but the words were already bursting from her lips.

'I did?'

'I'm ashamed to admit that it hadn't occurred to me that it might be a good idea to try and please the female members of the delegation.' She looked at him sharply, but his expression was completely guileless. 'They were delighted to find that Longworth, Hart, Holtz and MacLean employs attractive, intelligent women in responsible positions.'

She stared at him intently, trying to find even a hint of laughter or condescension in his eyes. Because if that's what he was doing, by God, if he was playing her for a fool again...

'At any rate, I hope it's not too late to offer my thanks, Hannah.' He rose and offered his hand to her. 'I'll see to it that there's a note of commendation placed in your personnel file.'

She stared at the outstretched hand as if it were contaminated with poison. A letter of commendation was the adult equivalent of a nursery-school gold star! Even if he was foolish enough to think she could be bribed, he was far too intelligent to attempt to do it so cheaply.

Her gaze flickered to his face. He was still smiling, very pleasantly and politely, and all at once she understood.

The man was absolutely serious! What had happened at her door, those heated kisses, even her embarrassing response, had meant so little to him that he'd forgotten it. He'd set out to humble her, he'd succeeded, and that was the end of it. He had wiped the slate clean.

But it wasn't. He might have forgotten, but she hadn't. He'd kissed her. He'd taken her in his arms. He'd—he'd turned her world upside-down and left her to lie awake half the night thinking about the taste of his mouth and the feel of his body against hers...

'Hannah?'

She looked up, horrified.

'Are you all right, Hannah?'

'Yes,' she said. But she wasn't. Her mind was racing almost as swiftly as her pulse. Where had such ridiculous thoughts come from?

'Are you sure?' He came around the desk quickly and put his arm lightly around her shoulders. 'Here, sit down. You're as white as a sheet.'

'I'm fine,' she insisted.

'How about some water?' He looked at the glass on his desk, half-filled with water, and handed it to her. 'Here. Take a sip.'

Their eyes met as his fingers brushed her lips, rough against the soft flesh, and she looked quickly at the glass.

'Thank you,' she said, and put it to her lips.

'I hope you don't mind sharing the glass,' he said.

She looked up quickly, but his face was expressionless.

'No,' she said, and gave him a tiny smile. 'Not at all.'

She sipped at the water, not because she wanted it but because it seemed safer to do that than to try and understand what in heaven's name was going on. After she'd managed a couple of swallows, she handed the glass to him.

'That's better,' he said pleasantly. 'The colour's coming back into your cheeks.'

'Mr MacLean...'

'Grant,' he said, and smiled.

She looked at him. If she didn't confront him in the next few seconds, it would be too late. But how could she, without making herself look more foolish than she already felt? How could she make an indignant speech about an incident so meaningless to him that he'd already forgotten it?

'Hannah?'

Say something, she thought furiously. Dammit, Hannah, say something. Anything.

'It's just occurred to me...' He frowned. 'Are you ill because of something you had last night? The wine, perhaps?'

The wine. Of course. She seized on the thought the way a drowning man would grasp a bit of driftwood. They'd both been under a strain to begin with, he worried about Magda Karolyi, she about the act she'd been forced into. And they'd both had some wine. Too much, perhaps. He had been aggressive, and she had been abrasive. Yes. It made sense—more sense than going off half-cocked, making a scene and losing the best job she'd ever had.

'Hannah?'

She took a deep breath.

'I'm fine, Mr...' His brows rose. 'Thank you, Grant,' she said with a polite smile. Her hand closed tightly around the letter of resignation and she crumpled it up and stuffed it into her pocket. 'Really.'

'Good.' He rose to his feet and she did, too. 'Now, then,' he said, his tone brisk and businesslike, 'do you think you can manage to go through those files by one o'clock?'

She nodded as they reached the door to the outer office. 'Of course. I'll get right to it.'

'Perhaps you should take some aspirin.' He opened the door and stepped aside. 'You might be coming down with the flu. Everyone seems to be catching it.'

'I doubt it,' she said, her tone as pleasant and impersonal as his. 'I don't feel ill at all.'

'Tired, then,' he said.

'Yes. Just a little...'

The words caught in her throat. The expression on his face had not changed, but his eyes had gone dark and smoky, and all at once she felt that same light-headedness she'd felt when he'd taken her in his arms and kissed her.

'Didn't you sleep well last night, Hannah?' She didn't answer, and his smile tilted just a fraction of an inch, hinting at something intimate and shared. 'No,' he said, 'you didn't. And neither did I.'

His gaze swept over her face, lingered on her parted lips. Hannah held her breath. God. Oh, God...

'Hannah?' Sally rapped lightly against the half-open door and smiled brightly. 'Oh. Mr MacLean. Sorry to bother you, sir. I didn't realise you were in yet. I was going to ask Hannah if she wanted to take her coffee-break now, but if she's busy...'

Sally's words faded as Grant swung towards her, his face a cold mask.

'At this hour?' He frowned as he looked past the two women to the wall clock in the outer office.

Sally cleared her throat. 'Well, sir, those of us who get in early usually go to the lunch room for coffee and a Danish just about——'

'Spare me the details, please. I don't care what you have or where you have it, just as long as it doesn't interfere with your work. You will have the material I want on my desk by one, Hannah, won't you?'

Somehow, Hannah nodded. 'Yes.'

'Good.'

The door swung closed. Sally stared at it in silence, and then she gave a dramatic shudder.

'Brrr,' she said. 'The temperature goes down fifty degrees when he's around. Honestly, I don't know how you put up with it! Well, never mind. Listen, wait until I tell you what Betty said when she saw that nightgown...'

Hannah smiled faintly as she followed the other girl into the corridor, even managing to look as if she was listening to Sally's story and laugh when the other girl laughed. But she didn't really hear anything she was saying. She was, indeed, still caught in that moment when Grant had looked at her with the memory of last night burning deep in his eyes.

What might have happened if Sally hadn't come bursting in?

She dug into her pocket, and her fingers clasped the crinkled letter of resignation.

Go back into his office and give it to him, a voice within her whispered, go on, dammit!

'Here we are,' Sally said. She moved towards a platter of pastries laid out near a coffee urn. 'Which do you want? Strawberry or cheese?'

Hannah hesitated, and then she straightened her shoulders.

Don't be a fool, she thought, and she drew her hand from her pocket, balled up the letter, and dumped it into the wastebasket beside the lunch room door.

'Strawberry's fine,' she said. She gave Sally a big, beaming smile and hurried on.

CHAPTER FOUR

'HANNAH?' Hannah looked up. Sally was standing in the doorway. 'Got a minute?'

Hannah smiled, pushed back from her computer, and slipped her eyeglasses from her nose.

'Hello, stranger,' she said. 'I haven't seen you in days. Come in and visit for a while.'

The other girl made a face. 'Is he here?' she hissed. She made a great show of peering inside Hannah's office and checking the corners. 'I'm not putting one foot inside that room unless the coast is clear.'

'You're safe.' Hannah nodded towards the closed door between her office and Grant MacLean's. 'He's on the phone long-distance. I doubt if he'll surface again until after six.'

'*Long* after six. Doesn't he ever go home?'

'He's been working on the Hungarian thing.' Hannah gestured to the papers strewn across her desk. 'Tying it up has been endless.'

Sally nodded. 'So I gather. But you'd think he'd remember that you have a life to lead. When was the last time you left this place on time?'

'I can't remember,' Hannah said with a smile. She pushed back her chair and rose to her feet. 'Want some coffee?'

'Ugh.' The other girl grimaced. 'I'm on caffeine overload already. How about tonight?'

'What do you mean?'

'Are you working overtime tonight, too?'

'I don't think so. I'm pretty much caught up, and——'

'Great. A new club opened on the next street. One of the girls in Personnel said it's packed with cute guys. I told her we'd——'

'Sorry.'

'But you just said——'

'I said I wasn't working late. But——'

'You've got a date already?'

Hannah touched her tongue to her lips. The only date she had for tonight was with a warm bath and the latest Robert Parker mystery, but she knew from experience that telling that to Sally would be a mistake.

'Sort of,' she said with a little shrug.

'Great!' Sally smiled. 'It's about time you started stepping out a little.'

'I've been busy,' Hannah said evasively. 'School five nights a week doesn't leave time for much else.'

'I know. But you gotta remember that old saw about all work and no play making Jack a dull boy. Or Hannah a dull girl.' Sally smiled. 'I'll expect to hear all the details tomorrow.'

Hannah's smile was vague. 'Well...'

'Ah, I get it. This one's a hot date, and the down-and-dirty might be too steamy for my tender ears.' Sally laughed, and, after a second, Hannah laughed along with her. 'You have fun tonight.' Sally stepped into the hallway, then popped her head back into the room. 'And we'll double another time, OK?'

'Yes. Sure. Another...' the door swung shut '...time,' Hannah murmured, and then she blew out her breath.

Terrific. Now she was telling lies to Sally, but what else could she do? They'd known each other for almost a year, and the other girl still didn't understand that searching for the perfect soulmate was rather like playing blind man's buff. You'd find somebody eventually, but when the blindfold came off, what then?

'But what about sex?' Sally had said once, her tone careless but her eyes bright with questions. 'Don't you—you know, don't you get lonely?'

Hannah's cheeks had flushed but she'd answered honestly. 'No,' she'd said—but, of course, she hadn't added that sex lost its lustre when you felt nothing for the man in your arms. She had never been the sort of girl to get turned on easily anyway. Towards the end, her ex-husband had accused her of being frigid.

'You're a lump of ice,' he'd complained nastily, and she couldn't deny it. She had *felt* like ice, cold to everything, wanting nothing...

Until that night more than two weeks ago, when she'd stood in the hallway of her apartment building, fumbling in the darkness with Grant MacLean as if she were a randy teenager, for God's sake, as if——

Hannah drew a deep breath. Whatever had made her think of that? The incident had been a temporary aberration on both their parts, that was all, and whatever she'd imagined in those few last moments before Sally had interrupted them the next morning had been just that—imaginings. She had only to look at the way Grant had treated her since to know that.

Not that he wasn't polite, she thought as she bent over her work. He was. He was also cooler than ever, as if to make certain she understood that what had happened that night had meant nothing. When Mr Holtz offered a smile and a 'Good girl!' by way of complimenting her on how well she'd represented the firm at the reception, Grant made it clear it had not been he who'd praised her but some of the Hungarian women.

'Not Magda Karolyi,' he'd said, with a little smile, and Hannah had, after the barest hesitation, smiled in return.

'Hannah?'

She spun around. Grant was standing in the middle of her office, watching her.

'Oh!' She gave a breathless little laugh. 'You startled me.'

He nodded towards the files lying beside her computer. 'I take it you've finished with those.'

She looked from him to the scattered documents, then to him again. His face was expressionless, but she was sure she heard a note of irritation in his voice.

'No, no, I haven't.'

'But you're almost done?' She nodded. 'I hope so.' He frowned down at his wristwatch. 'In fact, I'd like you to stay and finish those tonight. I'm leaving, but——'

'You're leaving?'

He looked at her. 'Is there a problem with that?'

'No, sir, of course not. I just thought that, since you were leaving, I——'

'Ah. I see. You assumed that you could leave if I were. Is that correct?'

'Well...' She hesitated. Why was he looking at her that way, as if she'd said or done something that had infuriated him? Just a minute ago, she'd been thinking about how polite he'd been lately, and now——

'Come, come, Hannah, I'm not a villain.' He crossed his arms over his chest and gave her a smile that was all teeth. 'If you can't work late this evening, just say so.'

Hannah's brows rose. 'I didn't say——'

'If you have a heavy date, I certainly wouldn't expect you to break it out of loyalty to me.' Grant's mouth twisted. 'Or is it a hot date? I'm afraid I find it impossible to keep up with the vernacular.'

She stared at him. 'You were listening to my conversation with Sally,' she said incredulously.

'I must say,' he said, distaste visible in the narrowed dark eyes, 'I would have thought better of you.'

Her face flushed. 'That makes two of us. What right had you to eavesdrop on——?'

'For God's sake, you needn't make it sound as if I had a glass to the wall!' He strode briskly across the room and snatched a paper from her desk. 'I started out of my office to see if you'd gotten anywhere with this report, but you and she had your heads together in an exchange of girlish confidences.' He snapped the paper straight and glared down at it. 'I thought it best not to interrupt, even though——'

'I'd have preferred you had, instead of——'

'—even though you were gabbing away on time I'm paying for.'

'I was not "gabbing away",' she said coldly. 'As for what you think you overheard——'

'I'm waiting for your answer,' he said, his voice sharp as it interrupted hers.

Hannah stared at him. 'My answer to what?'

'Can you manage to get that report done, or will it interfere with your plans for tonight?'

'My plans for tonight are——'

'Spare me the details, please. Can you finish the report, or can't you?'

The bastard! Hannah's breasts rose and fell with the swiftness of her breathing. Who did he think he was, passing judgement on her private life? Or was it the fact that she had a private life that so enraged him? How dared he speak to her this way?

She stared into his cold eyes, then squared her shoulders.

'It will be on your desk before I leave, sir.'

And so would her letter of resignation by the week's end. There was no sense in kidding herself. She couldn't work for such an impossibly arrogant s.o.b. This was exactly how he'd behaved that night he'd dragged her off to the reception at the Mark Hopkins, as if he were in charge of her every breathing moment.

'In that case, you'd better phone your date and tell him you're cancelling your plans for the evening.'

She smiled through her teeth. 'That's unnecessary. He won't mind waiting an hour.'

Grant's mouth narrowed. 'Two hours, perhaps.' He turned and strode towards his office. 'Or even longer. That report won't be finished until I've read it and approved it.'

She stared after him. 'You said you were leaving.'

'I've changed my mind.'

'But——'

He swung around and faced her. 'Just get it done, please,' he said coldly. 'The sooner you do, the sooner we can get out of here.'

'Yes, sir,' she said. Her voice was every bit as cold as his, which was a miracle because she didn't feel cold at all. She felt hot with rage; what she wanted to do was snatch the damned report from her desk and hurl it at his head. 'Mr MacLean?'

He spun to face her. 'What is it now?' he demanded, and she smiled; at least she hoped that was what she was doing. It was hard to be sure, because her lips felt as if they were sticking to her teeth.

'You were right.'

'Right? About what?'

'About getting the phrase wrong,' she said. 'I had a hot date tonight, not a heavy one.' She spoke pleasantly, even though she was so angry that her heart was galloping. 'People stopped saying "heavy date" years ago.' She paused, just long enough for maximum impact. 'Before I was born, I think.'

She had the satisfaction of seeing his face colour before she turned her back to him, walked to her desk, and sat down before her computer. It took all her determination not to look around again. Instead, she began typing, very quickly and, she knew, very erratically.

But it worked. After a few seconds, she heard him mutter something under his breath, and then his door slammed shut. Hannah dropped her hands to her lap.

All right. It was time to do what had to be done. She would finish out this week, then hand in her notice.

One way or another, Grant MacLean was an impossible man to work for.

It took exactly an hour and ten minutes to finish the report. When she was done, she ran it off on the printer, read it thoroughly, then placed it neatly in a folder and rose from her desk.

She knocked at her boss's door, then opened it. His chair was turned so that he faced the window and the darkening sky. 'The report's ready,' she said stiffly as she made her way towards his desk. 'You said you wanted to——'

He swung towards her and she fell silent. He was on the telephone, his expression intent.

'Marilyn,' he said, 'for goodness' sake, what do I know about——? Just put it on my desk, Hannah. No, Marilyn. No, I'm not ignoring you. I——'

Hannah strode across the carpet and out of the door. Another woman, she thought coldly. Marilyn this time, not Magda. She stabbed a hand at her computer and the screen turned black. Perhaps he had a thing for women whose names started with the letter M, she thought as she yanked her jacket from the corner coat-rack and slipped it on, although why any woman in her right mind would——

'Hannah!'

She spun around. 'The report is on your desk,' she said tightly. 'I just put it there. You saw me do it.'

'I have the report,' he said, holding out his hand and showing her the folder. 'What I need to know is what time you're meeting your date?'

'My date?' She stared at him. 'My. . . ?' And then she remembered. 'Oh.' Her gaze flew to the clock on the wall behind him. It was almost half-past six. 'Uh—at seven.'

'I suppose it would destroy your plans completely if you phoned him and said you'd meet him at eight.'

Hannah's shoulders slumped. Of course. He'd said the report wouldn't be finished until he'd read and approved it.

'Well?'

She looked up. He was watching her coldly. For a moment she almost blurted out what he could do with this job, but then she reminded herself that she only had to get to the end of the week, put in a letter of resignation, and walk off with a good reference.

'No, sir,' she said evenly, 'it wouldn't.'

'Do it, then.'

She stared at him, waiting for him to give her some privacy, but he just stood there, glaring at her. Finally, she snatched up the phone and dialled her own number.

'Hi,' she said to the droning dial tone, 'it's me. Yes, I'm afraid I'm going to be even later than——'

'Please be brief, Miss Lewis.'

She looked up. Grant was watching her with that same expression of distaste on his face she'd seen there earlier. 'I would have thought better of you,' he'd said, as if she weren't a woman—but then, he didn't think she was a woman, did he? He'd made a point of telling her she was an office automaton.

Her spine stiffened. 'Yes,' she said into the phone, 'I'm disappointed, too, but I'll be there as soon as——'

Grant tapped his fingers on the desk. 'Whenever you're ready,' he said coldly.

'As soon as I can,' she said. She gave Grant a malicious stare. 'Oh, don't worry about that. If you're asleep, I'll wake you when I get——'

'Dammit!' He grabbed the phone from her hand and slammed it into its cradle. 'I haven't got all night,' he said, dropping the report on her desk. 'Now get your things together and——'

'My things?'

'I need your help.' Frowning, he glanced at the clock behind her. 'And I'm running out of time.'

Hannah stared at him. 'I have no idea what you're talking about.'

'I need your assistance.'

She folded her arms over her breasts. 'In the office or out of it?'

'Look here, Hannah——'

'Maybe you're forgetting, Mr MacLean, but we went this route before. And I've no intention of——'

'The stores close at eight, don't they?'

'The stores?'

'I've an hour to buy a suitable gift.' He thrust his hand into his hair and glared at her. 'Now, how the hell am I supposed to do that?'

'I don't know,' Hannah said coldly. 'Perhaps you should ask Marilyn.'

'I did. And she told me she didn't want to influence me—damn, but isn't that just like a woman?' He grimaced. 'She suggested I get your help.'

'Did she, really?' she said, even more coldly.

He nodded and, to her surprise, doubt darkened his eyes. 'Look, I know this isn't part of your job. Not technically, anyway. But I've no idea what's appropriate, and——'

'No,' she said, as she thought of last Christmas when he'd asked her to order chocolates and perfume for a handful of women with spare, elegant names, 'I'm sure you don't. That's my job, isn't it?'

'Exactly.' He gave her a little smile of relief. 'You're a woman, Hannah, you know about these things...'

Something cold clamped around her heart. 'I'm your assistant,' she said, 'which means that all I know about these things is that choosing them is part of my job.'

Grant's smile shut off as if someone had thrown a switch.

'Exactly,' he snapped.

'Exactly,' Hannah repeated, and she picked up her handbag and marched to the door.

When they reached the street, Grant paused and looked around. 'Where do you think we ought to start?'

Where, indeed? She had ordered the chocolates and perfume over the phone, but clearly this was to be a special gift, lingerie, perhaps, or jewellery, and suddenly she wanted no part of it. It was one thing to make impersonal purchases for faceless women but quite another to be asked to select a nightgown or a bracelet for someone named Marilyn. How dared she? How dared *he*?

'There,' he said, and, before Hannah could tell him he could go ahead and stumble through the next few moments on his own, Grant clasped her arm and drew her forward. He stopped just inside the doors of the shop. 'OK. Now what?'

Hannah spun towards him. 'Now you walk up to the counter. And you tell the clerk you need something black and filmy——'

'What?'

'Or gold and glittery, whichever you prefer, and—and...' Her angry words faded to puzzled silence as she looked past him. Plush tigers and lions roared silently from the far corner, just beyond a miniature train that raced in endless circles around a Lego city. Hannah frowned. 'This is a toy store,' she said.

Grant glowered at her. 'A toy store that closes in less than an hour. Now, where shall we begin?'

'I don't understand. Marilyn wants you to buy her a toy?'

'Marilyn wants people to jump through hoops,' he muttered as they made their way down an aisle crammed with toy trucks and automobiles. 'Tommy's birthday party is next Saturday, but my dear sister suddenly decided the family had to celebrate on the actual evening on which he was born.' His hand closed on her arm and he manoeuvred her towards a display of toy aeroplanes. 'Which means that I'm supposed to find the right gift and give it to him tonight.'

Hannah started to smile. 'Let me get this straight,' she said. 'Marilyn is your sister?'

'Marilyn is a thorn in my side,' he said, but the way he said it made it clear she was anything but that. 'How about something like this?' He had stopped beside an Erector set, bristling with a complex of motors and miniature winches. 'Do you think Tommy would like it?'

This time, Hannah permitted the smile to spread across her face. 'How old is Tommy?'

'Four. He's four.' Grant looked at her. 'The thing of it is,' he said gruffly, 'I don't really know a hell of a lot about kids.'

Her smile dimmed. 'No,' she said softly, 'neither do I.'

'It's not that I don't like them...'

'You needn't explain.' It was none of her business. Besides, she was sure she understood. Grant MacLean wasn't the sort of man who'd have very much to do with children. He was too busy, too dedicated, first to his career and second to the pursuit of his own pleasures. Perhaps that was what had gone wrong with his marriage. Perhaps his wife had wanted a real marriage, a husband who was home every night by six-thirty, and two or three jam-smeared children.

That was easy to understand, Hannah thought. She'd harboured the same dream herself, and it came back with special poignancy at moments like this, when she saw mothers and children laughing together, because she knew that that was all it ever would be, a dream. It was too late for her now; having a family was out of her grasp unless she married again, and she had no wish to do something so foolish. Let the Bettys and Sallys of this world do as they liked, but she——

'Well?' Grant was looking at her, his brow furrowed. 'What do you think? Would my nephew like this Erector set?'

'Four, you say?' Hannah smiled. 'He'll love it—in a couple of years. But I think I see something he'll love at first sight now.'

They emerged from the toy shop half an hour later, Hannah clutching half a dozen gaily wrapped packages, Grant toting an enormous stuffed lion. It had started to drizzle, which meant that every taxi that passed them was filled.

When an empty one finally appeared, Grant bustled Hannah inside, then climbed in after her.

'You don't mind if we share this cab, do you?' he said. 'I'll get out at Marilyn's, and you can continue on home.'

Hannah agreed. Sharing a cab wasn't a problem, especially after the past few minutes. Her anger at Grant had vanished. How could it have done otherwise, after an intense debate over the comparative merits of plush lions versus shaggy sheepdogs?

The lion's smiling face poked into her shoulder.

'Sorry,' Grant said, shifting the creature in his arms.

'That's OK.' She smiled as she stroked the tawny mane. 'I hope Tommy's pleased with his gift.'

'Yeah. Me too.' He chuckled. 'I never realised just how big this guy really was until we got him out of the store.'

The cab's tyres dipped as it hit a pot-hole, and the lion's soft black nose poked into Hannah's cheek.

'Hey,' she said, grabbing fiercely at its velvety ears, 'watch that stuff, lion!'

Grant grinned. 'See what I mean? He's huge.'

'Uh-huh.' She laughed as the lion flopped against her again. 'I knew I shouldn't have agreed to share this cab.'

Grant's smile vanished. 'Yes.' His voice was suddenly chill. 'I almost forgot—your young man will be getting impatient.'

'My...?' She caught her bottom lip between her teeth. 'Oh,' she said quietly. 'I—I suppose he will.' Hannah swallowed. 'About that,' she began, but Grant's uplifted hand cut her off in mid-sentence.

'Please. You don't need to explain your behaviour to me.'

The disdain in his voice made her glad she hadn't said anything more. She gave him a cool look, then turned and stared straight ahead.

'You're right. What I do is none of your——'

'But it is,' he said coldly. 'I've no desire to hear you justify yourself, but——'

'Justify myself? Why would I——?'

'—but,' he said grimly, 'your morality is very much my concern, so long as you're in my employ.'

She swung towards him. 'What?'

'You heard me, Hannah. If you value your job, you'll hand your lover his walking papers.'

Her face darkened with anger. 'That's ridiculous! You can't dictate what I do on my own time. You're my employer, not my keeper!'

'Perhaps you need a keeper!'

'Just who do you think you are?'

'I told you. I'm your employer, and I expect you to live with a certain amount of decorum, even if——'

'We're here, mister.'

They had pulled up outside a handsome white brick house. Grant glared at Hannah, then at the cabbie, who was watching them in the mirror, a bored, I've-heard-it-all-before look on his face, and then he threw open the door and stepped on to the pavement. He shifted the lion to one arm as he dug out his wallet, and Hannah took small but satisfying pleasure in how ridiculous he looked with the big, tawny head propped against his shoulder.

'Think about what I've told you,' he said, bending down to the open window. 'And make your decision accordingly.'

'Grant!' A woman came hurrying from the door of the white brick house. When she reached Grant, she put her arm around his waist and offered her cheek for his kiss. 'You finally got here. I was beginning to lose hope.' She grinned. 'And just look at what you brought with you,' she said, patting the lion's head. 'Tommy's going to adore it!'

Grant's frown lessened. 'You think so?'

'I know so.' The woman linked her arm through his. 'See? I was right—you knew just what to get him after all.'

He shrugged almost grudgingly. 'Well, I can't really take the credit, Marilyn. It was my assistant, Hannah Lewis, who——'

'Miss Lewis?' The woman, a smaller, softer version of Grant, leaned down and peered into the cab. 'Is that you in there?'

Hannah nodded and forced a smile to her lips. 'Yes.'

'Honestly, Grant, where are your manners?' His sister flung the door open. 'Come on out, say hello, and join the party.'

Hannah shrank back in the seat. 'No. No, thank you. I—I——'

'She has to get home.' Grant's voice was harsh. 'She has someone waiting for her.' He gave Hannah a cold look. 'Isn't that right, Hannah?'

'Uncle Grant!' Grant turned just as a little boy flew down the steps. His face softened, and he bent and caught him in one arm. 'Mommy said you'd be here.' The child's face lit with pleasure. 'Is that lion for me?'

Grant nodded solemnly. 'He sure is. Do you like him?'

Tommy threw his arms around the creature's neck. 'I love him! Did you pick him out all by yourself?'

Marilyn laughed softly. 'The kid knows his uncle.'

Grant ruffled the boy's hair. 'Well, I had a little help.' He motioned towards Hannah, still seated in the taxi. 'From that lady.'

Tommy leaned down and looked in the window. 'Aren't you gonna come have some birthday cake?'

'No,' she said, 'I can't.'

'Please?' he asked solemnly, and, once Hannah had looked into his round blue eyes, what could she possibly say except 'yes'?

CHAPTER FIVE

THE party was a very small one, with only Tommy, his parents, Grant and Hannah present. There was cake and ice-cream, and balloons in the shapes of animals, and Hannah quickly realised that she needn't be concerned that the coolness between Grant and herself would spoil the festivities.

The spotlight was firmly on Tommy, thanks not only to his doting parents but to his Uncle Grant, as well. The boy was generous with his affection, and Grant more than returned every bit of that love to his nephew, with an openness and warmth that amazed Hannah.

Within minutes, he had cast off his jacket and rolled up his shirtsleeves so he could sprawl on the carpet and help Tommy build a castle of blocks. It ended with man and boy engaged in a fierce battle over who could demolish the castle the quickest—and laugh the hardest. Mean MacLean indeed, Hannah thought incredulously. Who'd have believed it?

Grant's sister slipped to her side and smiled. 'Grant and my son have a special relationship,' she said softly.

Hannah smiled back. 'So I see.'

Marilyn sighed wistfully. 'It's just too bad he hasn't a family of his own. He'd make a wonderful father.' She looked at Hannah. 'Have you children, Hannah?'

Hannah shook her head. 'No. No, I haven't.'

'Ah. You're not married, then?'

'No. Well, I was. But——'

''annah?'

Hannah looked down. Tommy was tugging gently at her skirt. Her expression softened as she squatted down beside him.

'What is it, sweetheart?'

The child handed her one of the candle-holders from his cake, a tiny blue plastic teddy-bear smeared with icing.

'For me?' Hannah asked, smiling.

The boy nodded solemnly. Somehow, he'd got the idea that she had given him her very own lion. Now he was offering a gift in its place.

'So's you won't be lonely,' he said.

A swift, fierce pain clutched at Hannah's heart. She wanted to sweep the child into her arms and bury her face in his neck. Instead, she reached out and brushed the curls back from his forehead.

'Thank you,' she said gravely, 'I certainly might have been lonely without my lion, but now——'

'It isn't necessary to patronise the child, Hannah.'

She looked up quickly. All the warmth had fled from Grant's face. He was watching her coldly and she recoiled, almost as if he'd slapped her in the face.

'Grant!' His sister stepped forward, but it was too late. Hannah had already risen to her feet.

'It's getting awfully late,' she said, trying desperately to look anywhere but at the dark, angry face looming above her. 'I—I really must be going.'

'Nonsense,' Marilyn said briskly, but Grant's voice cut sharply across hers.

'I told you,' he said as he pulled on his jacket, 'Miss Lewis has someone waiting for her.' Their eyes met. 'And we wouldn't want to keep her any longer.'

He insisted on phoning for a cab and seeing her home. He gave the driver her address, then sat back and folded his arms across his chest. They rode in silence; when they reached Hannah's house, she almost sprang from the taxi, but not quickly enough. Grant was right behind her.

'You don't have to see me up.'

'Afraid your boyfriend will get the wrong idea?'

Her eyes flashed with anger, but she said nothing. It was clear she would not get rid of Grant unless she let him play this charade through, and so she spun on her heel and strode into the building and up the stairs.

When they reached her door, she turned and faced him.

'You told me to think things over,' she said.

Grant nodded. 'And?'

'And,' she snapped, 'I quit.'

His face tightened. 'I expected that.'

Hannah lifted her head in defiance. 'I'll give you two weeks to find a replacement. In return, I'll expect a month's severance pay and a letter of recommendation.'

'Fair enough.'

'You don't know the meaning of that word.'

He clasped her shoulder as she began to swing away from him. 'Tell me the truth,' he said gruffly. 'Is there really a man waiting for you tonight?'

Hannah's heart gave a lurch. He was standing much too close to her, and she didn't like it. There was something about standing this way, in the dark, with the door at her back and Grant's body just brushing hers, that made her feel—trapped.

No. Not trapped. She felt—she felt...

'Well?' he demanded. 'Is there?'

She stared at him in defiance. Her fury made her want to assure him that there was, but all at once she knew there was something more at stake here, something she couldn't quite understand but couldn't quite fight against, either.

She blew out her breath. 'No.'

'Then why...?'

'Because you had no right to speak to me as you did. Because I'm tired of you behaving as if you're God. Because——' To her dismay, her eyes filled with tears and she swung away.

'Why are you crying?' Grant caught hold of her again and turned her to face him. 'Dammit, Hannah——'

She wrenched free of his grasp. 'Look, I don't know what game it is you're playing, but——'

'Don't you?'

Their eyes met. Hannah's heart gave an uncomfortable little kick.

'You're wasting your time,' she said as she dug her keys from her purse. 'I'm not interested.'

'Really.'

'Yes. Really. Prepare yourself for a shock, Grant. There are women in this world who can get along very nicely without a man to muck up their lives!'

He laughed. 'There are men who feel the same way.' His hand closed over hers as she stabbed her key into the lock. 'Me, for instance.'

She looked up at him. 'Please, Grant, don't treat me as if I'm a fool. I've been working for you for five months, remember? I've seen your appointment calendar, I've taken your calls... You're hardly a candidate for woman-hater of the year!'

He smiled tightly. 'I like women well enough. For certain things, anyway. It's just that I've stopped thinking of them in terms of forever after.'

'I'm sure that news has broken a lot of hearts,' she said coolly. 'Now, if you'll excuse me...'

His fingers curled more closely around her wrist. He moved nearer and she backed away instinctively, until her shoulders were pressed against the closed door to her flat.

'What is it, Hannah? Have you forgotten that there's some value to male-female relationships?' He smiled. 'For instance,' he said, and before she could move or turn away he bent and ran his mouth lightly over hers.

Hannah caught her breath. 'Don't!'

'Why not?' he whispered. 'Hell, if you don't need this sort of thing, then it shouldn't upset you.'

There was something very wrong with his reasoning, but there was something even more wrong with what was happening to her as his mouth, cool and smooth as silk, drifted across her skin. Her breath was quickening and a warmth that was soft and almost liquid was spreading through her bones.

'Grant?'

He gathered her into his arms. 'What?' he said thickly, and his mouth dropped to hers again. She was waiting for the kiss. Her lips opened to his, and his tongue stole slowly into her mouth.

He murmured her name as he slid his hands under her jacket. She felt the heat of his fingers against her midriff, then on the underswell of her breasts, and when she groaned he caught the sound in his mouth and deepened the kiss.

'Hannah,' he whispered. His hands slid up her throat and framed her face. 'Hannah...'

She spun away from him and turned the doorknob. Grant could have stopped her, she knew that. He was quick and strong, and she was no match for him physically. But he let her go, and when she slammed the door and fell safely back against it, trembling, her one coherent thought was that it was a damned good thing her relationship with Grant MacLean was about to be history.

Hannah felt some concern about going to work the next morning, enough that she thought about phoning the office and telling Grant she'd changed her mind about giving him two weeks to replace her.

But she needed a decent reference if she was to get another job anywhere near as good as this one, and she knew Grant far too well to think he'd give her one if she walked out and left him in the lurch.

And so she showered and dressed as if this were any other morning, even though her stomach was in knots. She clipped back her hair, dabbed a pale lipstick over her mouth, and strode out of the door, prepared to meet whatever lay ahead.

It was almost anti-climactic to find that nothing did. There was a note on her desk, terse and to the point. Grant had been called to Washington, DC on business. He would return by the week's end. In his absence, she was to deal with the following items.

He had left her a month's worth of work to be done in four days, which came as no real surprise. She'd half assumed he'd make her final two weeks hell, either to make sure she had no time to sneak off for interviews with prospective employers or simply to please himself. Well, she thought as she settled in at her desk, that was fine. The school at which she'd studied ran its own placement office. One phone call would set up several interviews when she was ready.

In the meantime, she'd work as hard as she always had.

On Wednesday morning, Sally appeared in the doorway, bearing an envelope embossed with the Longworth, Hart, Holtz and MacLean logo.

'For you,' she said, handing it over with a flourish. 'Special from Mr Longworth himself.'

It was an invitation to a formal dinner the firm was giving on Friday evening for the Hungarian delegation.

'Just look at that,' Sally said, rolling her eyes. 'Can you imagine?'

Hannah couldn't, but when she tried, very politely, to tell that to Mr Longworth, the old man put his arm around her shoulders.

'Didn't MacLean tell you that the Hungarian ladies were impressed with you?'

'He mentioned it,' she said. 'But——'

'Well, then,' he said with a paternal smile, 'what's the problem, Hannah? Surely you're not going to let them down.'

Surely you're not going to let us down, was what he meant. She was tempted to tell him that it wouldn't matter, that in another ten days she'd be gone, but she thought better of it. She was still an employee of the firm. Besides, such an evening might prove beneficial. Who knew what kinds of employment contacts she could make?

If only it didn't mean spending an evening pretending to be pleasant to Grant, especially under the cold scrutiny of his partners, not to mention Magda Karolyi.

'It's especially important you attend, Hannah, now that MacLean's stuck in Washington.'

Her head came up. 'Is he?'

Mr Longworth nodded. 'I've just been on the phone with him. The trade commission's giving us a bad time. He won't be back until Monday.'

Hannah smiled. 'In that case,' she said, 'how can I say no?'

Mr Longworth insisted she buy a dress and charge it to the firm. 'It's not an expense you need assume, Hannah,' he said in kindly tones, and Hannah knew he was suggesting, in the most diplomatic way possible, that she might not own something suitable for such an elegant evening.

'And he's right,' she told Sally, who'd agreed to help her find a dress.

'Let's get something that'll knock their socks off,' Sally said as they poked through the rack in a little shop during the lunch hour.

In the end, they compromised, choosing neither the calf-length black jersey Hannah had selected nor the tiny, sequin-studded concoction Sally sighed over but, instead, a dress in chocolate velvet, with a short skirt and a deep V of a bodice.

Too short—and too deep, Hannah thought now, as she stood before her mirror on Friday evening. The dress was stunning, she had to admit that. It was beautiful and feminine; it even softened the look of her oversized glasses. But there wasn't enough of it. The neckline was cut down to there, the skirt up to here—and, in between, the velvety fabric clung to her every curve.

She glanced at the clock. The firm was sending a limousine for her, but she had ten minutes to spare. Surely there was something else in her closet, a dressy suit or——

The doorbell pealed.

Hannah blew out her breath as she hurried to the door. 'You're early,' she said as she yanked it open. 'And I'm sorry, but you're going to have to wait while I change my...' Her words trickled to silence. It was not a uniformed chauffeur who stood in the doorway, it was Grant, dark and tall and incredibly handsome in a black dinner-jacket.

'Good evening, Hannah.'

'What—what are you doing here?'

He smiled. 'I've come to take you to the party.'

'No.' She shook her head. 'No, that's—it's impossible. You're in Washington.'

'I assure you,' he said, his smile broadening, 'I'm here. May I come in?'

She stepped back, speechless, and he moved past her, his arm just brushing hers, bringing with him a faint drift of cool night air and lemony cologne.

'I don't understand,' she said slowly. 'Mr Longworth said——'

'I managed to tie things up sooner than expected.' She watched as he strolled slowly through the tiny living-room, pausing now and then to glance at one of the framed prints on the wall or to brush his hand lightly over some of the little glass animal figures she collected. 'No lions, I see,' he said with a little smile.

Hannah blinked. 'No what?'

'Lions. Which reminds me, Tommy sends his love and says Brian is just fine.'

'Brian?' she echoed foolishly.

'Brian the Lion.' Grant swung towards her and smiled. 'Marilyn swears she had nothing to do with naming the creature.'

Lions. Tommy. Marilyn. It was all to much to comprehend, especially when she was still trying to deal with the fact that she was, apparently, going to have to spend the evening in Grant's company.

Or did she?

Hannah smiled brightly. 'Well,' she said pleasantly, 'I'm glad to see you made it back in time for the dinner party.'

He smiled again, but differently this time, in a way that made her breath suddenly uneven. She felt the weight of his gaze as it swept over her, lingering on her face, her breasts, the long length of leg visible beneath the ridiculously short skirt of her dress.

'Are you?' he said softly.

'Yes. Of course.' She cleared her throat. 'I was only going because you weren't. Well, I mean, Mr Longworth felt it was important that one of us be there, but now that you're back——'

'Get your wrap, Hannah.'

Her smile wavered a little. 'You didn't let me finish,' she said. 'You're here, you see, so I——'

She fell silent as he moved towards her. When he reached her he stopped, looked into her eyes and gave her a cool smile.

'Do you still want that letter of reference?' he asked.

And that was how she came to be standing on a terrace outside a small, exclusive club in Sausalito, overlooking the Golden Gate Bridge and the San Francisco skyline, several hours later.

It was midnight, which meant the evening was almost over and she could afford to relax. Somehow, perhaps because she'd come to the party accompanied by Grant, her role this evening had taken on a new dimension and she'd found herself at the centre of one group or another all night, with Grant at her side, his arm lying lightly around her waist or her shoulders. Now, with few guests remaining, she'd finally been able to slip away for a quiet moment and a breath of cool night air.

She felt as if she'd been riding a roller-coaster. You could shout and scream, but the ride kept going. The best you could do was hang on for dear life—and perhaps find, at the end, that you'd had fun.

She sighed as she leaned her arms on the railing. And she had, that was the amazing thing. She'd been stiff with indignation at first, but how indignant could you be when you were at a party where the guests were charming, the conversation stimulating, the food delicious . . . ?

And the man at your side was the object of every other woman's desire—not just Magda Karolyi, who'd managed one frosty smile then kept her distance, but all the women who'd been here tonight. She'd seen the admiring glances they gave Grant, the flirty little smiles.

Hannah gave herself a mental shake. Well, of course they'd be attracted to him. He was good-looking, attentive, charming—but no one knew the other side of him, the one that was brash and demanding, confident to the point of being arrogant. That was why she was here, wasn't it? Because he'd forced her into coming?

But she was happy she had. It had been fun, being with all these people. Grant's presence hadn't had a thing to do with it. He'd just—he'd just——

'Well, that's the last of them.'

Hannah spun around at the sound of Grant's voice. 'The last of what?' Her heartbeat quickened. There was no denying that he was the best-looking man here tonight, perhaps the best-looking man she'd ever seen. There was nothing conventionally handsome about him. His face was hard, almost harsh, but there was character in every plane. His body was hard, too; you could tell that even though he was dressed in that elegantly tailored dinner-jacket.

'Here.' He held out one of the glasses. 'Go on, take it. You look exhausted—the brandy will pick you up.'

'Or put me down,' she said, smiling as she took the glass. 'It's been a long day.'

'And a longer evening?' He came to stand beside her, one hand clasping the railing as he looked out at the bridge.

She wanted to answer yes, it had been. But what harm was there in admitting that she'd had a pleasant time? None, now that the night was almost ended. In just a moment or two, she'd go back into the room, and the limousine would whisk her away.

Hannah drew a breath. 'Not really. Actually, I—I had fun.'

He turned and leaned his back against the balcony railing. 'Well,' he said softly, 'that must have taken a lot. Admitting that you had a good time to the bastard who blackmailed you into coming here.'

She flushed. 'Yes. And, just because the evening turned out well it doesn't mean that I——'

'No. I didn't think it would.' He smiled. 'You're a very prickly woman, do you know that?'

'Not prickly. Just—independent.'

'Yes.' His gaze swept across her in almost impersonal assessment. 'An admirable trait in a woman.'

Hannah looked at him. 'I find it hard to believe you mean that.'

He smiled again. 'Oh, but I do,' he said softly. 'Independence is a virtue, much to be desired.'

She could sense a growing electricity in the air around them, and suddenly Hannah wanted nothing more than to be safely back in her flat. She put down her glass.

'It's late, Grant. I'm sure my driver would appreciate knowing his duties were at an end.'

'I dismissed him.

Hannah stared at him. 'You did what?'

He looked at her. 'I said, I dismissed him. I'll see you home myself.'

She stiffened. Was that how he thought this evening would end?

'You shouldn't have done that,' she said coldly.

He smiled at her over the rim of his brandy snifter. 'Marilyn tells me Tommy talks about you non-stop.'

The sudden change in conversation caught her up short. 'What?'

'My nephew. It seems you made quite a hit with the kid.'

Some of the rigidity eased from Hannah's shoulders. 'Well,' she said softly, 'he's a sweet little boy.'

Grant nodded. 'I agree.' There was a moment's silence. 'Why didn't you and your ex-husband have children, Hannah?'

'That's an awfully personal question, don't you think?'

He took a sip of his brandy. 'We didn't have them—my ex-wife and I—because she didn't want any.'

Her eyes widened. 'Didn't want children?' she repeated foolishly.

Grant shrugged his shoulders. 'It turned out she was more dedicated to her career than to what she called my old-fashioned ideas of home and family.'

'But you did? Want a family, I mean?'

'Very much.' His smile twisted. 'Why do you look at me that way, Hannah? Is it so impossible to imagine me as a father?'

Hannah shook her head. 'I—I don't know. I never thought——' Her words drifted away. Yes, she thought, she could easily imagine him as a father. He'd been tender with Tommy, and very caring...

'You didn't answer my question,' he said. 'Why didn't you have children?'

It was none of his business. But his own honesty prompted hers.

'My husband was—I suppose the kindest thing I can say is that he wasn't ready to settle down. We talked about having a baby, but...' She smiled a little. 'It's probably just as well we didn't, considering. But——'

'Yes?'

It was her turn to give a self-deprecating shrug. 'I suppose I'm old-fashioned, too. I think a child's best off with two caring parents, not one. It's just that sometimes—sometimes...'

'Go on,' Grant said softly.

Still, Hannah hesitated. This was too personal a conversation to be having, especially with this man. But she understood it. There was something about discussing things late at night after a party with strangers...

'Sometimes,' she said quietly, 'I think I should have had a baby then, when I had the chance.'

'Surely you'll fall in love and marry again?'

Smiling, she shook her head. 'I've had enough of both. It took me a long time to get over the failure of my marriage.' Her tone was quiet but filled with strength.

'But I did, and now I'm quite content with my life as it is.'

'Uncomplicated,' Grant said, and Hannah nodded. 'Independent.' She nodded again, and this time he nodded too. 'So, as much as you'd like a child...'

'As much as I'd like that,' she said with a quick, false smile, 'the odds of having one range from slim to non-existent.'

'There are other ways,' he said, his voice suddenly soft.

'Adoption? Yes, I know single women adopt all the time. But——'

'I meant, other ways to have one's own child. Other methods.'

Hannah flushed. 'Test-tube babies, you mean?' She shook her head. 'No, I wouldn't want to do that any more than I'd want to adopt. It would be selfish. My child would have no father and only a part-time mother. I'd have to work, leave my baby in someone's care...'

'Suppose you could overcome those difficulties.'

Hannah looked at him. 'Overcome them?'

'Yes. If your child could have a father who loved it and bore all the paternal responsibilities without dragging you into a marriage, if he could properly support you and the child——'

She smiled, puzzled. 'This is an interesting late-night exercise in a game of "what if," Grant, but——'

'Hannah.' Grant put down his brandy, took hold of her shoulders, and turned her to him. 'I've been thinking about something all evening.'

He stepped closer to her, she saw the sudden tightening of his mouth, and just that quickly she knew that everything that had gone on tonight, even the serious talk of the last few months, had all simply been prelude to what came next.

The Seduction of Hannah. The thought made her catch her breath, not with distress but with—with...

'I want to leave,' she said, starting blindly past him, but he caught hold of her hand and drew her back.

'Hannah——'

'I told you, Grant, I'm not interested.'

'Dammit,' he said gruffly, 'will you please shut up and listen?'

'Why? You have nothing to say that I want to hear.' Her chin rose. 'I am not going to bed with you. I am not going to become your lover, or your mistress.'

'What I was thinking about,' he said, his eyes locked on her face, 'was what we were discussing. The less orthodox means of having babies.'

The abrupt change in the conversation baffled her. 'What?'

'You heard me, Hannah. I was thinking about other ways of having children.'

She stared at him. 'Adoption?'

'No,' he said impatiently, 'not adoption.'

'Test-tube babies, then? Is that what——?'

He stalked away from her, slapped his hands on the railing, then turned and stuffed his hands into his pockets, and Hannah thought, incongruously, that it was the first time she'd ever seen Grant MacLean anything less than fully in command.

'I don't understand,' she began, but his voice, harsh as steel, sliced across hers.

'There's no easy way to put this,' he said, 'so I'll just get to it.' He took a breath. 'What I'm trying to say, Hannah, is that I want you to bear my child.'

CHAPTER SIX

HANNAH had lived in San Francisco all her life, which meant that she paid little attention to fog-shrouded, chilly mornings. Everyone knew the sun would soon burn the mist away and reveal the city in all its shining brilliance.

But on the morning after Grant's incredible proposition the mist curling outside the windows of her bedroom seemed greyer and more determined than usual, as if it was planning to settle in and stay.

Not that she gave a damn, Hannah thought as she shoved back the blankets and got out of bed. It was a Saturday, and she had nothing more urgent to do than wait for the janitor to show up to fix a leaky bathroom tap—and draft her letter of resignation from Longworth, Hart, Holtz and MacLean.

Shivering, she pulled on a black cotton turtle-neck shirt and beige corduroy trousers, then stomped to the kitchen and switched on the light. The room was not cheerful in the best of circumstances. Ageing appliances, white tiled walls and a grey linoleum floor lent it a dilapidated look, one Hannah's landlord was unwilling to change and would not permit her to change on her own. Now, in the cold glare of the overhead fluorescent, with tendrils of mist pulling at the window, the place looked positively grim.

Almost as grim as she felt, Hannah thought as she opened the cupboard and plucked a canister of coffee from the shelf. But then, who wouldn't feel that way after what she'd endured last night?

Last night, she'd described her ex-husband as a man not ready to settle down. That was true enough—as far as it went. In fact, he'd been self-centred to the point of not giving a damn for anyone but himself. Still, compared to Grant, he'd been a saint.

Hannah dumped coffee into the filter, slapped the pot on the stove, and switched on the burner. She leaned back against the sink, arms folded across her chest, her lips a narrow line. What was it about her that drew such selfish men? Although there was one major difference between her ex and Grant MacLean. Her husband had done little more than drift towards what he wanted. Grant—Grant went after it with the determination and subtlety of a ballistic missile.

What MacLean wanted, MacLean got. And what he wanted just now was an heir.

Hannah snatched up the pot as the water hissed and boiled over the top. She filled her mug with a thick, oily liquid, then marched out of the kitchen and into the living-room.

The nerve of the man! The unmitigated gall of him!

'I want you to bear my child,' she said aloud, her voice mimicking his nastily with deep tones and arrogant self-confidence.

She took a mouthful of the coffee, shuddered, then took another.

'And I want you to go straight to hell, Grant,' she said, but after a moment her shoulders slumped.

It was, of course, the only proper rejoinder. Hannah sighed and sank down into the sofa, the mug of bitter coffee clutched in her hands. The only trouble was, she hadn't had the presence of mind to make it. All she'd been able to manage was an open-mouthed stare, a snort of laughter, and an incredulous, 'You what?'

'I've given the matter a great deal of thought,' he'd said, and then he'd opened his jacket so he could tuck his hands into his pockets, and he'd begun pacing the terrace, not nervously but quite leisurely, the way he did at work when he was laying out ideas for a case. He'd droned on and on, his voice calm, his tone reasoned, but Hannah hadn't heard a word beyond the first ones. She'd been thinking, instead, that Grant had gone crazy.

After a moment, she'd decided that she had to be as insane as he for listening to such nonsense.

'Goodnight, Grant,' she said, interrupting what must have been a brilliant presentation, because he gave her a look that would have killed if it could.

'Have you heard one thing I said?' he growled and, while she wondered if it would be better to placate this madman or try to restore his sanity, he marched to where she stood and clasped her tightly by the shoulders. 'You haven't, have you?'

Was it a joke? Who knew what passed for humour these days?

'I said, I want a child.' He gave her the sort of expectant look she'd seen him give opponents after he'd put an offer on the table that he thought just and fair. 'I'm quite serious, Hannah,' he added, and when she looked into his cool eyes all hope of an explanation fled.

He *was* serious, she thought with a start.

'Yes, that's right.' He smiled tightly as he read her face. 'I want a son.' He paused in that familiar posture that she knew meant he was marshalling his thoughts. 'A daughter will do too, of course. I suppose it makes more sense to say that I simply want a child.'

'A child,' she repeated inanely.

'Yes,' he said impatiently. 'A child. Surely that's not an unusual desire.'

A child, requested from a woman he held in sufferance, requested as coolly and calmly as if he were asking her to put in an extra hour at the office? No, she thought dizzily, no, that wasn't an unusual desire at all.

'I'm not getting any younger,' he said. 'I'll be forty soon, and if I'm going to be a father—a real one, not the armchair version—I should do it now.'

He went on talking, about how she wasn't to think this was a spur-of-the-moment idea, about how he'd done considerable research into the new, non-traditional family, while her mouth dropped further and further open, until finally the reality of his words penetrated—

really penetrated—and a white-hot rage swept through her.

He wanted a baby. Surely she'd agree? It was simply a business deal, all very legal and cold-blooded, involving his overblown ego and requiring only a battalion of laboratory flasks—and her womb. They would conceive a child in a test-tube, she would deliver it—and turn it over to him.

The bastard! The rat! The——

'Hannah?' he said sharply. 'Are you listening?'

'Yes,' she snapped, twisting out of his grasp, 'I certainly am listening—to the most insulting, the most egotistical, the most hideously outrageous——'

'Dammit, you're *not* listening!' A pair of vertical lines appeared between his eyebrows. 'I'm not suggesting marriage or any of that nonsense. I'm suggesting——'

'I know what you're suggesting,' she said as she elbowed past him. 'Where's the telephone?'

'Hannah, dammit, wait!'

But she hadn't waited, she'd called for a taxi, and when it arrived she'd been waiting on the pavement, and her flat-out refusal to let Grant see her home while both the cabbie and the doorman pretended uninterest had finally brought a flush of anger to his face.

'Take the lady to her door,' he'd snarled, shoving a fistful of bills at the driver, and then he'd turned and marched back into the building—and that, Hannah thought now, as she rose from the sofa and made her way to the kitchen, was the last she would ever see of Grant MacLean. She would be as crazy as he was if she showed up for work on Monday morning.

Her jaw tightened as she refilled her mug. Forget the letter of resignation. What she'd send was a telegram, terse and to the point, demanding that he write her a proper reference and have it hand-delivered at once.

And he'd damned well better. If he didn't—if he didn't, she'd go straight to Longworth, Hart and Holtz and tell them exactly what kind of slimy creature their esteemed partner was, and to hell with all his threats.

The doorbell shrilled. Terrific. Just what she needed right now. The janitor, with his cheery smile and propensity for small talk. He was a nice old man, and ordinarily she enjoyed the chat that invariably accompanied each visit.

But not today, she thought as she hurried to the door and threw it open, not...

Grant, his dark hair wind-ruffled and fog-damp, wearing faded denims, a leather jacket, and a grim expression, stood in the doorway.

'I'm coming in,' he said, not '*may* I come in', or even I'd *like* to come in'—but then, he wasn't the kind of man who ever asked those questions. It was all moot anyway, Hannah thought furiously as he used her stunned moment of surprise to shoulder past her into her small living-room, where he stood facing her, his hands shoved deep into his jacket pockets, his legs slightly apart, every inch of him taut with determination and tightly contained anger.

Hannah drew a deep breath, leaned back against the open door, and folded her arms over her breasts.

'You wasted your time coming here. I've nothing to say to you.'

'All you have to do is listen.'

She shook her head. 'There's nothing to listen to.'

'Don't be a fool,' he snapped. 'I made you an absolutely legitimate offer, and——'

'Legitimate?' She gave a forced laugh. 'Is that what you call an offer to—to——?'

'To bear a child. What's the matter, Hannah, can't you say the words?'

'What do you think I am? A—a machine that's just been waiting for someone to come along and—and drop in a coin?'

He made a sound that might have been a laugh. 'What a charming analogy.'

Colour flooded her face. 'Get out!'

'Not until you've heard me out. Last night——'

'Did you hear what I said? Get——'

She shrank back as he crossed the floor and grabbed her by the shoulders.

'Not until you listen.'

'No, Grant, *you* listen. I am not going to—to become pregnant with your child. I'm not going to—to be a brood mare, to give you a baby because you want one and——' She made a strangled sound as one of her neighbours suddenly appeared at the head of the steps. The woman looked at her, eyes wide, and Hannah's colour deepened. 'We were—we were just talking about a—a TV show,' she said wildly.

'No, we weren't,' Grant said calmly. 'We were discussing the pros and cons of having a baby.'

Hannah turned and retreated into her living-room. When she heard the door slam shut, she swung around.

'I'm only going to say this once,' she said, her voice trembling. 'Either you leave now, or I'll——'

'We talked about having children, remember? You said you wanted to be a mother.'

'I did not!'

'You did, dammit! You said you want——'

'*Wanted*,' she said tightly. 'That's the word, Grant. I *wanted* a child, once upon a time, when I had a husband and a wedding-band and—and all the silly dreams I'd...' Her voice quavered. This was what he'd done with his stupid comments and his insensitivity, damn him; he'd dredged up all the hopes she'd buried along with her marriage. Hannah took a deep breath. 'That's beside the point anyway. What you're suggesting has nothing to do with motherhood.'

His brows lifted. 'Hasn't it?'

'For God's sake, Grant, having a baby is more than—than biology.'

He nodded, his eyes fixed on her face.

'It's—it's seeing your baby's first tooth, and—and watching him take his first step,' she said. 'It's staying up all night when he's ill, it's changing diapers and cleaning up spills and——'

'I still don't see the problem.'

Hannah threw up her hands in dismay. 'It's a life that's part of you. How can you even suggest that I'd—I'd be willing to give birth to a child and—and hand it over to you?'

He snarled a word that turned her face red. 'My God, is that how little you think of me? Did you really imagine I'd ask you to give birth to a child, then give it away?'

'Well, isn't that what——?'

'No,' he said coldly, 'it isn't.' He unzipped his jacket, stripped it off, and tossed it on the sofa. 'Is that coffee I smell?'

She blinked. 'Yes.'

'Where's the kitchen? Through there?' He turned before she could answer and strode into the next room. Hannah followed after him like a sleepwalker. By the time she arrived, he'd already found a mug and filled it with coffee. She watched as he tossed half of it down, shuddered, then poured a refill. 'You weren't paying attention to me last night, Hannah.'

'I was. You said——'

'I said, I wanted us to have a child. *Us*. You and I. I said I would pay all your expenses, that I'd sign papers making me responsible for the child's support until it's done with college or medical school or whatever.' He took another swallow of coffee. 'And,' he said with emphasis, 'I said he—or she—would reside with you, that I would support you, that you would raise the child and in every way be the kind of mother you've always wanted to be.'

Hannah reached behind her for a chair. Had he said all this? Not that it mattered. His proposal was out of the question. Perhaps he thought that if he explained it this way it would be more palatable, make him seem less a robot and more a man.

'Hannah.' Grant's voice softened. She looked up and found him watching her carefully. 'Do you understand? I certainly wasn't asking you to bear a child and have no other involvement with it.'

'It doesn't matter. What you're describing——'

'Yes, I know.' He thrust his fingers into his hair and raked it back from his forehead. 'I mean, even though we both think that love and marriage are phoney excuses for people who just want sex——'

Hannah flushed. It was an assessment she couldn't argue with. That was certainly all her ex had wanted from their relationship.

'Still, there's a certain validity in staying within conventions.'

'Exactly. I'm glad you see how I feel, Grant. After all, having a child isn't——'

'I mean,' he said, frowning, 'it's one thing to agree to have a baby without being bound by outmoded rules for its conception, but——'

'What are you talking about? You just said——'

'I'm talking about having a child without falling back on the old-fashioned ideas that control reproduction in our society, Hannah. They wouldn't apply if we were to go any further with this idea.'

Why did everything this man said make her blush? She was too old to blush so easily; she wasn't a teenager who turned red at the mention of sex.

And he was talking about doing it *without* sex, for God's sake; he was talking about a procedure that was about as sexy as—as going to the gynaecologist.

She looked up. He was watching her narrowly, and suddenly she thought she knew how a mouse must feel as a cat herded it into a corner. She was being manipulated, with great delicacy but also with great determination, and the feeling was frightening.

She got quickly to her feet. 'But we're not going any further,' she said, 'so there's no point in having this discussion, is there?'

'It occurred to me, too,' he continued, as if she hadn't spoken, 'that you might feel that our child had no legal father. You'd be wrong, of course; he would bear my name and I'd acknowledge him to the world—but...' He frowned and thrust his hands into the back pockets of his jeans. 'I never considered that you and the child would have to bear the onus of its being born out of wedlock.' He smiled for the first time, and Hannah thought crazily that he suddenly looked very young and even more handsome than usual. 'Even though that's a dated concept in some circles.'

'Grant,' Hannah said weakly, 'this is—it's all fascinating. And—and I suppose I should be flattered, I mean, that you'd ask me to—to have your child, but——'

'So, what I've decided is that there's only one way to deal with these issues. We'd still have the child as we've discussed.'

'Without—without falling back on the old-fashioned ideas that surround reproduction?'

'Yes.' He paused and, for some reason, her heart did, too. 'But we'd do it within the framework of a marriage.'

Marriage.

'Marriage?' she repeated incredulously.

'Well, followed by divorce, of course. It's the only solution, Hannah. Surely you see that?'

She stared at him in disbelief, trying to read something, anything, in his expression, but the only sign he gave that something unusual might be happening was the movement of a little muscle, knotting and unknotting in his jaw.

'It would solve all our difficulties.'

'But—but——'

'I'd draw up a contract,' he said quietly, his eyes fixed on her face. 'So many months for you to become pregnant...'

'Pregnant,' she whispered, falling back into the chair.

'Of course, it's possible that might not occur, in which case I wouldn't expect you to remain locked in the relationship forever.'

God! She had heard him discuss business deals with the same amount of emotion.

'And if we weren't successful I'd support you until you got your life organised again.'

Was he making some sort of bad joke? No, she thought as he swung towards her, no, he was serious. Her heart banged against her ribs.

'As for living arrangements—my apartment is very large. It's a triplex with a view of the Bridge—well, the point is, there are eighteen rooms, so you'd be assured of privacy. You'd have your own suite. As for what happens if our endeavour proves successful——'

'Do you know how insane this is?' she whispered.

His scowl deepened. 'Don't interrupt me.'

'But——'

'If things did work out,' he said, his voice cutting across hers, 'we'd have to agree to stay married for a time. For the child's sake, of course.'

'Grant——'

'Three years, perhaps. That's enough for him to form an attachment to us both, yet be able to adapt to our separation.' His eyes flashed to her face, and a tight smile twisted across his lips. 'You could manage three years as my wife, couldn't you?'

She said nothing. After a long moment, Grant turned and strode to the sink.

'This is terrible coffee,' he said briskly, dumping the thick black liquid down the drain.

Hannah felt torn between the desire to laugh and to cry.

'I know. I—I don't know how you managed to drink any of it.'

'And this is the world's most depressing kitchen.'

She did laugh this time. 'I couldn't agree more. My landlord——'

'We can't possibly talk here.' He swung towards her. 'Why don't we go out and have some breakfast? I had a law-school professor who wanted to make it illegal to discuss contract terms on an empty stomach.'

'But we're not——'

'Hannah.' He came towards her, clasped her shoulders, and helped her gently to her feet. 'I'm starved, hungry enough to eat and drink almost anything—except for that coffee.' He smiled. 'What harm can there possibly be in joining me for a bite to eat?'

All the harm in the world, Hannah's brain shrieked, but anything was better than being trapped in these too-confining rooms while Grant spun his crazy story of babies and make-believe marriages that were all mixed up with a life she had once dreamed of.

And, before she could think, she gave him a little smile and agreed that there certainly couldn't be any danger in joining him for breakfast.

He had come to her flat in his car. She had never seen it before, and when it turned out to be sleek and black and very close to the ground she thought that it suited him, that it had about it an aura of danger and risk and masculine aggression, just as he did.

He settled her into the seat beside him, his fingers brushing hers as she and he locked their seatbelts at the same time. A tremor shot through her, and he frowned.

'Is something the matter?' he asked.

She shook her head and folded her hands tightly together in her lap.

'No, nothing.'

He nodded, then stepped on the accelerator. The car shot away from the kerb, its tyres hissing against the wet roadway. Hannah's hair was loose—at weekends, when it wasn't necessary to worry about looking professional, she rarely wore it back—and the wind, coming through the open windows, whipped it about her face.

'Shall I close them?' Grant asked, his hand hovering over the buttons that controlled the electric windows, but she shook her head.

'No,' she said, 'the breeze feels good.'

And it did, she thought as they crossed the Golden Gate Bridge, the high arches trailing wisps of fog. The wind tugging at her hair made her feel wonderful, free and wild in a way she hadn't felt in years.

She glanced at Grant, seated beside her, and suddenly she wondered what would have happened if they'd met years ago, if it had been he and not her ex-husband who'd given her her first kiss, who'd touched her intimately for the first time. There'd have been none of this cold, clinical talk of contracts and artificially conceived babies then; they'd have come together naturally, in each other's arms, with warmth and laughter and passion.

She turned her head away sharply. What was the matter with her? She didn't feel anything for this man. He was the impossible bastard who had cost her her job. Now his arrogance had taken him into uncharted depths: it had made him propose a mockery of a marriage so they could have a child, a child born not through an act of love but through a medical marvel, and she, fool that she was, had let him babble on about it.

'Listen, Grant,' she said sharply, and she angled towards him, the demand that he take her home on her tongue. But they were already turning into the parking area outside a restaurant with a red-tiled roof and a soft Spanish name, and with a sigh Hannah decided that it might be easier and safer to tell him she'd had enough of his nonsense in a place where they'd be surrounded by other people.

Maybe then he'd give in gracefully and take her home instead of hammering away at her like a trial lawyer.

They were seated at a round table in a glass-enclosed courtyard where succulents and brightly coloured flowers grew around a softly bubbling foundation. Grant ordered for them both, things she usually loved—*huevos rancheros* and cornmeal tortillas, fresh mango and steaming cups of hot coffee laced with rum and chocolate. But every mouthful caught in Hannah's throat. All she could think of was the insanity of Grant's request, and her even greater insanity in letting him, even for a minute, think she'd been willing to listen. She should have—she should have thrown him out the door of her apartment, she should have——

'You have the right to know about the failure of my marriage.'

She looked up, startled. Grant was leaning towards her, his expression intent.

'I made it sound last night as if it were all my ex-wife's fault.' He frowned. 'But I have to bear the blame, too. We were wrong for each other, and I should have seen that. The marriage was a colossal mistake.'

Hannah cleared her throat. 'Well,' she said briskly, 'well, that's—that's very interesting. But——'

'But the experience did teach me something,' he said, almost sternly. 'I learned that marriage isn't for me. I like my life just as it is. The freedom, the time to dedicate to my work...'

And to your women, Hannah thought, and a strange lump rose in her throat.

'It's just that, as the years pass, I look at other men with their children...' He cleared his throat. 'I don't know why I'm telling you all this, Hannah—except that I think you feel much the same, don't you?'

'Yes. But——'

'That's why you're the perfect woman for this—this undertaking. Do you see?'

Hannah shook her head. 'No. I don't see. I don't see at all.'

'Of course you do,' he said impatiently. 'You just aren't ready to admit it.'

She stared at him. He was impossible. Impossible! He had set his sights on something, and nothing would stand in his way, not even common sense.

But she knew how to deal with a man like this. You just shook your head, pushed back your chair, and walked away.

He caught her hand as she started to rise. 'Sit down, Hannah!'

'Let go!' she spat as she fell back into her seat. 'I don't know why I let you talk me into——'

'What are you afraid of? This won't be a real marriage, dammit! And our divorce will be quick and painless.'

'It's out of the question.'

'Why? Give me one good reason.'

'I don't have to.'

'Humour me. Tell me why you won't accept my offer.'

'Well—well, there's—there's something cold-blooded about having a child through such—such artificial means.' Colour rushed to her cheeks. 'Not that I'm for a minute suggesting——'

'I suppose it does sound cold-blooded. But it would be a child that both of us wanted, and we wouldn't be hurting anyone.'

'Look, if this is such a great idea, why not trot it out for someone else?' Her eyes met his. 'We both know there's no scarcity of women in your life.'

'That's true enough,' he said calmly. 'But you're special.'

There it was again, that stupid little lift of her heart. 'Indeed?' she said, as calmly as he.

Grant nodded. 'Aside from feeling as I do about marriage and children, you're bright and resourceful. And I've seen you with Tommy; I know you're good with kids.'

Why did it sound like a shopping list? Hannah shifted uneasily. 'So? None of that's unusual.'

'We don't bore each other. And we find each other attractive. Physically, I mean.'

She forced herself to go on looking straight at him. 'Even if that were true,' she said stiffly, 'what would such things have to do with an arrangement like the one you're proposing?'

He smiled. 'I know you think I'm crazy, Hannah, but I'm not crazy enough to commit myself to the company of a woman I find dull or unattractive.'

She stared at him helplessly. Why was she letting this continue? She wasn't going to agree, no matter what he said.

'And you're independent.' His smile faded, and his expression grew businesslike. 'That's vital. The last thing I'd want is to enter into an agreement like this with a woman who might decide that married life was what she'd always wanted.'

The cold words stung, although there was no reason why they should. If, by some miracle, she ever thought about marrying again, it would be to a gentle, predictable man, one just the opposite of Grant MacLean.

'Well, that's certainly not a description of me,' she said with a chill smile.

'No. It's not.' He leaned forward. 'And yet, for all those admirable traits, Hannah, you're alone. Think about the years stretching ahead. How will you fill them?'

Her eyes flashed to his. 'That's a cheap trick, trying to make my life sound empty when it's——'

'You'll have that little flat, a couple of holidays in Hawaii or Las Vegas, and your job. Is that enough?'

'I have friends.'

'And sooner or later every last one of them will be caught up in Parents' Day and Scouts,' he said with cruel directness. 'Where will that leave you?'

Without warning, tears rose in her eyes. She twisted her hand free of his, shoved back her chair and got to her feet.

'I want to go home.'

'Hannah——'

'Did you hear me? Take me home. Now.'

She turned and rushed from the restaurant, the tears blinding her as she made her way past the fountain and the flowers and out to the car park. The bastard! She had a perfectly comfortable life, she had everything she needed and wanted . . .

Grant's hands closed on her shoulders and he spun her towards him. 'It hurts to face the truth, doesn't it?'

'Damn you,' she whispered, 'damn you to hell, Grant MacLean. You've no right——'

'No right to suggest something that will give both of us happiness without the pain neither of us wants?'

She scrubbed furiously at her damp eyes. 'Who do you think you are?'

'I *know* who I am, Hannah! I'm a man who's looked at life and found he's riding on a fast train bound for nowhere, the same as you.'

'Oh, yes,' she said furiously. 'And you've found this magic, simple solution——'

'It *is* simple.'

'It isn't. What you're suggesting is—is——'

'Logical. Practical. Sensible.'

'You left out "embarrassing". Or haven't you considered what people would think of such an arrangement?'

Grant's brows rose. 'I don't give a damn what people think.'

'I do. We live in different worlds, Grant. Maybe you can make your own rules, but I...'

'Are you thinking about your family?'

Hannah shook her head. 'I don't have a family. My parents died a few years ago.'

'Well, then?'

'Well, there's—there's the office. Your partners.'

He smiled. 'I'm far too valuable for them to say anything about how I lead my life. As long as it's nothing illegal or scandalous, they'll tolerate whatever I do and say nothing.'

'And what about *your* family?'

'There's only Marilyn.' His smile broadened. 'And she'd be so happy to hear I've decided to settle down that she wouldn't ask any questions if I announced my engagement to—to Magda Karolyi.'

Hannah laughed despite herself. 'That's some recommendation.' Her smile faded. 'And then there's Sally, and the girls at work, and——'

'Then we don't have to tell anyone anything.'

'No. It wouldn't work.'

Grant smiled. 'You're underestimating us. We can make the world see us as just another man and woman who took a good look at each other one day and decided they liked what they saw.'

'That's easy to say, but——'

'Watch,' he whispered, and before she could take a breath he drew her into his arms and parted her lips with his, his tongue slipping along the soft inside of her mouth. His mouth was warm, his kiss gentle, but suddenly she felt heat building deep within her, spreading through her blood and into her limbs. A tremor went through her. Grant made a soft sound in his throat and gathered her to him. It seemed a long, long time before he clasped her shoulders and put her from him.

They stood staring at each other, Hannah as shaken by the sudden, unreadable darkness in Grant's eyes as by the power of his kiss. But then he smiled and the darkness dissolved, and she knew that what she'd seen in his eyes had been satisfaction.

'We could fool the world if we had to,' he said. 'Couldn't we?'

Their eyes met again. She could have it all—a home and security and a baby to love, with no man owning her heart who could break it.

Grant clasped her shoulders. 'Dammit,' he said in a fierce whisper, 'say yes.'

It was insane. It was impossible.

His hands framed her face, and her heart almost stopped beating. Was he going to kiss her again? She couldn't let that happen.

'Hannah? Will you at least think about it?'

Anything, she thought desperately, anything to make him stop looking at her that way, to make him let go of her.

'Yes,' she whispered, 'all right, I will. I——'

A smile swept across his face. 'I knew you'd see it my way,' he said triumphantly.

She stared at him in horror. 'Grant, no! I only said——'

He drew her into his arms. 'I promise you, Hannah, you'll never regret this decision.'

By the time he'd finished kissing her, she was beyond thinking anything.

CHAPTER SEVEN

THE rain had picked up, and the fog that had earlier curled so picturesquely over the Golden Gate Bridge was now a treacherous, blinding hazard. Hannah could see taut concentration in Grant's every movement as he nursed the car forward.

Surely this was no time to try and tell him that he'd misunderstood what she'd said at the restaurant. She would wait until they reached her flat, and then she'd ask him in after he'd taken her to her door, make some tea, force him to listen.

But, for the very first time, Grant didn't take her to her door. He pulled to the kerb, sprang out of the car, and came around to her side.

'I'm sorry, I can't see you up,' he said briskly as he helped her from the car. 'I have some errands to run, and I promised Marilyn I'd stop by for a while. You understand.'

She stared at him. 'But we have to talk!'

'We will. At the office, I promise.' He frowned. 'Unless you'd prefer not to go upstairs alone . . . ?'

Hannah laughed. 'Don't be silly. I always——'

'Good.' Grant dropped a light kiss on her upturned face. 'I'll see you, then.'

She watched open-mouthed as he hopped into his car and drove off into the fog, and then she turned slowly and made her way indoors. All right, then. She'd phone him.

But her calls went unanswered. Grant's brisk, recorded voice kept telling her she'd reached his number and saying, 'Kindly leave your name, number, and a brief message.'

How could you leave a message saying you would not go through with a mockery of a marriage nor agree to bear a child according to a contract? At midnight, she gave up and went to bed. They would settle matters in the office, she thought, and fell into a troubled sleep.

On Monday morning she went to work earlier than usual, but Grant was already there, waiting for her. She had wondered how to tell him he'd made a mistake. How would he react? Would he be angry? Would he try and insist they'd reached agreement?

Grant didn't give her any time to find out.

'You're fired,' he said, without preamble, almost the very moment she slipped off her coat.

Hannah stared at him. 'I'm what?' she said. The coat slid through her fingers and fell, unnoticed, to the floor.

He smiled a little. 'Perhaps I should say that you've just given notice. As of this moment, you are my fiancée, not my legal assistant.'

'But—but I'm not——'

'We have a lot to do,' he said. 'And not a hell of a lot of time to do it in.'

'Grant.' She drew a breath. 'Listen to me. You can't just fire me. I need my job.'

'Don't be silly. You do not "need" your job.' He took her coat from where she'd dropped it and slipped it around her shoulders. 'Keep that on,' he said. 'We're going out.'

She looked after him in bewilderment as he walked to his office.

'Of course I need my job,' she said, following after him. 'I have expenses to meet.'

Grant opened his calendar, glanced at it, then closed it and put it down.

'What expenses?'

'What do you mean, what expenses?' she said with a unsteady smile. 'Rent on my apartment. Groceries. Utilities. Clothing. A dozen other things.'

He looked at her and smiled. 'You won't be paying rent,' he said reasonably. 'You'll be living with me.'

'That's what I want to talk to you about,' Hannah said quickly. 'About what I said when we were leaving the restaurant—what you thought I said, I mean.'

'My partners all said to tell you they're very happy for us both, by the way.'

She stared at him. 'You—you told them?'

'Of course. Marilyn's happy, too.' He grinned. 'More than happy, actually. She's ecstatic.'

'Marilyn knows, too?' Hannah asked in a shaky whisper.

Grant nodded. 'Oh, and one other thing.' He strolled to the wardrobe on the far side of the room. 'I've made wedding arrangements for next Thursday. Thursday afternoon, actually.' He smiled as he pulled on his topcoat. 'At one o'clock.'

She sank down on the edge of a chair. 'Next Thursday? Grant! My God! You—you shouldn't have...'

'Is there something wrong with Thursday?'

Hannah looked up. He was watching her with an expectant smile, as if he'd asked her if she'd mind working late that evening.

'The day's not the problem. It's——'

'Good.' He frowned. 'Actually, there is one more detail. I've notified your landlord that you'll be giving up your flat. And I called your bank and——'

'What?' She got to her feet and stared at him. 'What did you do?'

'I called your bank.' He took her elbow and walked her out of the door and down the corridor. 'I've arranged for some funds to be transferred into your account. I've no idea what you might wish to buy for yourself before our wedding, but——'

'I don't want your money!'

'Don't be silly.' Frowning, he pressed the call button for the lift. 'There must be purchases you'll want to make before next Thursday.'

'Not a one,' she said coldly.

'That's nonsense, Hannah.' The lift doors slid open and they stepped inside. 'You need a trousseau. Luggage. Clothes for our honeymoon. Whatever.'

'This is impossible!' She stared at him as the lift dropped. It was a high-speed one, and Sally always joked that it got to the ground floor before her stomach did. Hannah had never agreed—until now. 'I'm trying to tell you,' she said sharply, 'we don't have to go on a——'

'Of course we do. You're the one who wanted our marriage to look as normal as possible, remember?'

'Well, yes, but I never meant——'

'Don't look so stricken,' Grant said, smiling at her as they stepped into the lobby. 'I haven't taken over completely.

She glanced up at him as he took her arm and led her from the building, his step just brisk enough so she had to stretch her legs a bit to keep up, the feel of his hand on her elbow light but subtly controlling.

'Haven't you?' she said, her tone chill.

'Of course not.' His smile broadened. 'After all, I'm going to let you choose your own engagement-ring.'

Hannah came to a stop. 'Don't be ridiculous,' she said. 'I don't need an engagement-ring.'

'Of course you do,' he said smoothly. His hand closed on hers and he drew her out to the street. 'What would people think if I didn't give you a ring?'

She looked at him in dismay as he hailed a taxi, then handed her inside.

'But you said—you said you didn't care what people thought...'

'And you said you did.' He leaned forward and gave the driver an address, and then he sat back and smiled at her. 'It's all part of the same thing, Hannah. You can understand that.'

'No,' Hannah said, 'actually—actually, I don't understand it. We—I only said——'

'You expressed a concern about appearances. And the more I thought about that concern, the more I realised you're right.'

'I am?' she asked, puzzled. She could count the number of times he'd thought her 'right' on the fingers of one hand, and still have fingers left to hold a teaspoon.

'There's no harm in creating the appropriate illusion,' he said.

'Wait a minute,' Hannah said. Her voice was shaking. 'Just wait one damned minute, Grant!'

'What's the matter?' He looked at her. 'Have I done something wrong?'

'Wrong? *Wrong*?' She gave a sharp bark of laughter. 'You—you've taken over my life, Grant! You've announced our wedding to your partners, to your family——'

'I was simply trying to expedite things, Hannah.'

'You—you called my landlord and cancelled my lease——'

'Well, I'm an attorney. I thought it might be better if I handled it.'

'You contacted my bank...' Hannah drew a shuddering breath. 'Dammit, Grant, I am not your property!'

'You're going to be my wife,' he said, pleasantly enough but with a hint of steel lying just below the surface.

'Being a man's wife doesn't make a woman his—his chattel!'

'I agree. But it does give him the responsibility of taking proper care of her.'

'Being responsible for someone does not grant you the right to make decisions for them,' she said sharply. 'I have made my own decisions for many years, and I'm not about to stop now!'

He looked at her for a moment. 'All right,' he said softly. 'Suppose we say that, from now on, I'll take your opinions into consideration when making decisions that concern us both. How's that?'

'It's not good enough. I'll expect you to discuss things with me...' Hannah's voice faltered in bewilderment. 'I mean, I'd expect you to do that. If—if I were going to marry you.' She drew a deep breath. 'But—but I'm not.'

She waited, expecting—expecting what? she thought, as her eyes searched his face. Anger? Rage? Something like that. Instead, he scowled and thrust his hands deep into his pockets.

'I see,' he said.

'You misunderstood me the other day,' she said quickly. 'I never said I'd agreed to your idea, only that I'd think about it.'

'And, having thought about it, you've decided you don't want a child after all.'

'No. Oh, no.' She put her hand on his arm. 'Of course I want a child. But——'

'You've decided that you wouldn't want a child of mine, then.'

'No. Grant, it's nothing like that. I——'

'Are you concerned that I might renege on my obligations? Is that the problem, Hannah?'

Hannah shook her head. 'Of course not. I know you'd—you'd give me a fine child. And I know you'd be a good father to it.' Her eyes filled with tears and she put her hand to her breast. 'As for me—oh, Grant, you can't know what having a baby would mean to me. It would be—it would be...'

'A dream come true,' Grant said softly. 'Then come dream with me, Hannah. We can make this work. I know we can.'

Their eyes met and, for once, Hannah was silent. Come dream with me, he'd said.

How could she argue against such a wonderful offer?

The 'appropriate illusion' of an engagement-ring turned out to be a seven-carat emerald surrounded by diamonds. Grant had said she would choose her own ring and she did—after he'd specified emeralds of a certain cut and size to the smiling sales clerk in Tiffany's.

'Do you like it?' he asked softly, once the ring was on Hannah's left hand.

Did she like it? Hannah stared into the deep green heart of the stone. He might as well ask if she liked the sun or the stars. They were all beautiful, all burning with unearthly fire.

'Hannah?'

She looked up at him. He was watching her with a peculiar intensity that made the breath catch in her throat.

'Yes,' she said. 'Of course I like it. It's—it's very beautiful.'

He nodded. 'I thought emeralds, to bring out the green in your eyes,' he said, so softly that she wasn't certain she'd heard him. Their glances met, and for a heartbeat Hannah wondered why she had ever thought she'd never seen as deep a fire as the one gleaming in the heart of the emerald. But then Grant turned away, and when he spoke to the sales clerk his tone was brisk and unsentimental.

'We'll need wedding-bands, too,' he said. 'Wide ones, I think, in yellow gold.'

When they had finished, he led Hannah out to the street and into another taxi.

'Neiman-Marcus,' he said to the driver.

Hannah gave a little laugh. 'Grant,' she said, 'really, don't you think we should go back to the office? I've work to finish.'

'I told you,' he said sharply, 'you are not working for me any longer.' He drew a breath, and when he spoke again his tone was soft and indulgent. 'You need a dress to be married in, Hannah. I know it's bad luck for the groom to see it, but——'

'But in these circumstances, what does it matter?' Her voice was flat. Did he really think he needed to remind her of that?

Grant looked at her in silence, and then he nodded. 'Exactly,' he said crisply. 'I'm glad you see it my way.'

Was there another way to see things but Grant's? Hannah didn't think so. Moments later, standing in the exclusive store's dress department, she felt like a bystander as he took even the selection of her wedding-dress out of her hands.

'I think—something practical,' she said to the sales clerk, 'a wool suit, perhaps, in grey or beige. And nothing——' She glanced at the obviously expensive clothing artfully draped in a nearby display and flushed. 'Nothing too extravagant.'

Grant laughed softly and slid his arm around her waist. 'What the lady really wants,' he said, 'is a dress or a suit in a pale shade to complement her own colouring.' His arm tightened around her. 'Something special, to wear on our wedding-day.'

The woman beamed. 'Of course, sir. *Madame*? If you'll come with me, please?'

The dresses and gowns were dazzling, as were the discreet price tags attached to them.

'No, that's much too expensive,' Hannah kept saying, until suddenly Grant was there, brushing aside her protests, choosing a lemon-yellow suit, a royal blue cashmere shirtwaister, and a pink silk coat-dress.

'Try them all,' he said. Hannah started to protest, but that touch of steel was in his voice again and in his eyes, as well, and she turned on her heel and marched into the dressing-room.

'*Madame* is fortunate to have such a handsome and generous fiancé,' the saleswoman murmured.

Hannah smiled politely. Yes. Grant was handsome. And generous. And he never took 'no' for an answer. He would always get what he wanted, despite what he'd said a little while ago. Hadn't he proved that with her from the beginning?

'*Madame* looks lovely,' the sales clerk purred. 'Shall we step outside and show your fiancé this outfit?'

Hannah let herself be led out of the dressing-room. Was she really ready for this? She'd all but handed herself over to Grant for the next three years—and three years was a long time. A very long time.

'. . . three. Yes, I think so, don't you, darling?'

She blinked and looked up. Grant and the saleswoman were both smiling.

'Don't I what?' Hannah asked.

Grant's smile broadened. 'I said, three's a lucky number, don't you think?'

She stared at him. 'Grant——'

'It is, absolutely. We'll take all three.' He flashed Hannah a dazzling smile. 'That way, you can surprise me when I see you coming down the aisle next Thursday.'

When they were alone again in a taxi, she turned quickly to him. 'What aisle?' she said in an angry whisper. 'Surely you haven't made arrangements for a church wedding?'

Grant shook his head. 'No.' His mouth twisted. 'I thought that might be going a little far.'

'Well, I'm glad to hear——'

'Marilyn suggested we hold the ceremony in their summer place, about an hour south of here.' He frowned when she didn't respond. 'Hannah? Is there a problem?'

Her fingers brushed across the florentined gold of her engagement-ring, tugged restlessly at the glowing emerald. Yes, oh, yes, there was. What was she letting herself in for? Marriage was a mistake in the best of circumstances—she knew that better than anyone. But to enter into one this way, knowing it was temporary and without meaning...

Well, not exactly without meaning. They would have a child, if things worked out. But the marriage itself would never be real. They were living a falsehood, deluding everybody and even playing at deluding each other.

'Is there?'

She looked at Grant. His voice had gone flat; she knew that he sensed her hesitation.

'I—I'm not sure,' she murmured. 'Maybe—maybe things are moving too quickly. I need time.'

'Time for what?' His tone was chill.

'Well...just, you know. Time.' She turned the engagement-ring on her finger, around and around.

'Perhaps you'll feel more comfortable when you see the contract.'

She looked at him. 'You mean you've drawn it up already?'

Grant nodded. 'Yes.'

A wave of dizziness swept through her and she suddenly felt as if she were standing at the edge of a precipice.

'When?'

A little smile curved quickly across his mouth. 'Sunday. I had some time on my hands, so...' He shrugged. 'It's at the office.'

They reached the building in the middle of the lunch hour, which meant that it was quiet and the offices empty. Hannah thought the receptionist gave her a funny smile as Grant hurried her past, but there was no time to dwell on that. Within minutes she was seated in his office, not on the straight-backed chair where she'd sat so many times during the past five months but on one of the leather couches. Grant sat opposite her, watching as she tried to read through the legal document he'd stuffed into her hands.

'Whereas Hannah Lewis and Grant MacLean have agreed to enter into a state of legal matrimony...'

She read on and on, until the dry words ran together in a blur, and then she looked up at him.

'It's longer than I expected.'

He frowned. 'It's a contract, Hannah. I've tried to cover all the contingencies. What do you think? Have I left anything out? Do the provisions satisfy you?'

Hannah's brow furrowed as she bent over the contract again. What *could* she think? She had studied the basics of law, but he was the lawyer, not she. There were phrases here she didn't fully understand, clauses and terms that were far too complex for her.

'Basically,' Grant said, 'the contract spells out what we've already agreed on verbally. We'll give ourselves three years to conceive——'

'Three years? Three years was how long we said we'd stay together, after our baby is born.'

'Of course. And we'll give ourselves the same amount of time to get you pregnant.'

A flush rose the length of Hannah's body and travelled swiftly to her cheeks.

'Must you say it that way?' she said stiffly.

Grant's brows lifted. 'Why? Does the word offend you?'

'It just sounds so—so personal.'

His voice was suddenly rough. 'Don't worry, Hannah, there's nothing personal about this. I'm aware of your reservations.'

She nodded. 'I know you are. I just...'

'Do you want to have your own attorney look it over?'

She almost laughed. 'I haven't got an attorney. Besides, I'm not questioning the document. I'm sure you've done it properly. It's just——'

'Then sign it.' She looked up. His voice was soft as silk; he was smiling and holding a pen out to her.

The breath whooshed from her lungs, and she tossed the contract on the table between the couches and rose to her feet. 'Grant,' she said in an urgent tone, 'I've been thinking. Maybe—maybe we ought to—to back off a little. Think things through again.'

'No.'

She spun around and looked at him. He had got to his feet, too, and was standing with his arms akimbo, the expression on his face so hawk-like and implacable that a shiver of apprehension swept over her.

She swallowed drily. 'There's no rush, after all.'

'We made a deal, Hannah. You can't renege now.'

'I'm not trying to.'

'Then why do you want to delay our wedding?'

Our wedding. Our wedding. But it wasn't a wedding, it was a sham. It was a charade.

'I need time,' she said desperately. 'Please, Grant, surely——'

The telephone rang. They both stared at it, and then Grant snatched it up and barked an angry 'hello'.

Hannah turned swiftly for the door, pulled it open, and fairly flew into the safety of the outer office.

This was never going to work. Never. It was impossible. It was——

'Hannah?' She looked up. Sally had appeared in the doorway, and the instant she saw her face she knew what would come next. 'Oh, Hannah,' Sally said, tears glistening in her eyes, 'how exciting!'

'Sally.' Hannah took a step forward. 'Before you say anything, I want to tell you that—that——'

'I didn't believe it, at first, when Mr Longworth told me.' She dashed into the room, grabbed Hannah, and hugged her. 'Oh, my gosh, what a ring!' she said, dancing back a step. 'I'm so happy for you!'

'Sally. Wait. I'm not—we're not—nothing's really been—— '

'Mr Longworth said it would be all right if we closed down for the rest of the afternoon.' Sally grinned. 'None of us would get any work down anyway, considering.'

Hannah felt behind her for the edge of her desk, took a step back, then leaned against it.

'You and Mean Mac...' Sally slapped her hands to her mouth. 'Sorry,' she said with a little laugh, 'that just slipped out. When did it happen?'

Hannah waved her hand in the air. 'I—I don't know, exactly. It just—it just did.'

Sally nodded. 'I always knew he had to have a heart.' Her eyes widened. 'Oh, I'm sorry, Hannah. It's just that——'

'It's just that you're surprised.' Hannah nodded. 'I know.' She gave the other girl a shaky smile. 'Me, too.'

'Yeah, I'll bet. We're all so happy for you. We didn't have time to plan a party. A real one, I mean. But——'

'Oh, that's all right,' Hannah said quickly. She hesitated. 'Actually—actually, nothing's definite yet.' Sally's smile became a puzzled frown, and Hannah hurried on. 'The thing is, Grant and I haven't actually——'

'What my fiancée's trying to say,' Grant said as he stepped from his office and walked towards the women, 'is that we haven't quite agreed on the date.' He put his arm around Hannah and smiled down at her. 'I thought next Thursday, but she's afraid that won't give her enough time to get ready. Isn't that right, darling?' Hannah looked up at him, at those ice-grey eyes that were flashing a warning. He drew her closer into the hard warmth of his body. 'And I've been assuring her that there's not all that much to do. We've already given notice to her landlord, and I was just on the phone with that little girl from Estates and Trusts——'

'Patty,' Sally said helpfully.

'Patty, that's right. I've asked her to take your job as of tomorrow, darling.' His teeth flashed in a quick smile. 'You see? Everything has been taken care of.'

'And we've even managed to put together a shower for you,' Sally said brightly.

Hannah turned pale. 'A shower? A bridal shower?'

Sally smiled. 'It won't be a surprise, but then, they never really are, are they? A girl always knows she's going to have a shower when she leaves to get married.'

There was a silence. Hannah looked from her friend's shining face to Grant's glittering eyes. It was like being swept forward by a tidal wave, she thought; there was no way back and no way to turn.

'Would you excuse us for a minute please, Sally?' Grant said, and, without waiting for the girl's answer, he drew Hannah into his office and quietly closed the door. Once they were alone, he let go of her. 'You were about to sign the contract when that phone call interrupted us.'

'That's not exactly the way it happened,' Hannah said stiffly. She waited for him to say something, but he didn't. After a moment, she touched the tip of her tongue to her lips. 'Did you plan it this way? Getting Sally involved, so that the whole office would know and——'

'The contract,' he said, holding a pen out to her.

Hannah caught her breath. 'Grant—look, I know I agreed to—to...' She swallowed. 'But now I—I'm not certain——'

'Sign it, Hannah.'

His face was hard, his gaze unswerving. She waited a moment, then snatched the pen from his hand, stalked to the table where the contract lay waiting, and scrawled her name. When she was done, she tossed down the pen and turned towards him, her expression shuttered and cool.

'Satisfied?' she said.

A lazy smile spread across Grant's face. 'Very,' he said. Slowly, his eyes never leaving hers, he reached out and gathered her into his arms. 'Very,' he whispered, and then he drew her close and kissed her.

It was a long, unhurried kiss, a kiss that she knew was meant as confirmation of his power over her. It was nothing more than a pretence of passion, and yet Hannah felt the earth drop away from beneath her feet, felt the room spin around her. Heat shimmied through her blood, touching her everywhere with a sweet, fierce pleasure.

A discreet knock on the closed door drove them apart. 'Hannah?'

It was Sally. Hannah swayed on her feet, her only link to the planet the harsh pressure of Grant's hands on her forearms.

'I'll see you later,' he murmured.

She swung away from him, heart racing, and wrenched open the door.

'The party,' Sally began, and Hannah nodded and followed her into the hall and towards the lunch room and a celebration that was, in the best of circumstances, an ordeal to be endured, but was a special hell now that it was in her honour.

At least she didn't have to make any small talk. Sally did it all for her, chattering away non-stop about the fun of planning the last-minute shower, about how thrilled all the secretaries were, about how handsome Grant was.

Hannah kept nodding and smiling, but she wasn't really listening. She was thinking about how Grant had trapped her, wrapping her in a web of silk so fine no one but she would ever know it was there.

But she could survive that. When all of this was finally over, she would have what she wanted. A child. That was why she'd entered into this bizarre pact, after all.

Sally tugged at her sleeve. 'Wait until you see the nightgown we bought you.' She giggled. 'I'm not supposed to tell you, but it's really something! It's white and sheer, cut down to here and up to there——'

And Grant would never see it. It was little compensation, Hannah thought as she fixed a smile to her face and entered the lunch room, but it was something.

And it would have to do.

CHAPTER EIGHT

MARILYN HOWE plucked a microscopic bit of lint from Hannah's shell-pink skirt and sighed with pleasure.

'You're beautiful,' she said happily. 'Absolutely beautiful.'

Hannah looked into the mirror that ran the length of one wall in the Howe guest room. A stranger looked back at her, a stranger whose shiny chestnut hair fell loose to her shoulders, whose face was pale, whose doubt-filled eyes seemed enormous without their usual oversized glasses.

'I hardly recognise myself,' she murmured.

She looked so different, she thought uneasily. The emerald ring, flashing on her finger each time she moved her hand; the lovely, incredibly expensive pink dress that clung to her body with stylish grace; the contact lenses Marilyn had talked her into trying... All of it added up to a woman Hannah had never seen before.

The realisation was terrifying, but then, everything about this day was terrifying, for in just a little while she would become Grant's wife.

Hannah MacLean. Mrs Grant MacLean. *Oh, God...*

'Are you all right, Hannah?'

Hannah blinked and looked into the glass. No, she thought, while her heart galloped wildly, no, I'm not all right. I feel as if I've made a pact with the devil.

'Hannah? Do you want to sit down for a minute? Shall I send for Grant?'

'No!' Hannah drew a deep breath and forced a smile to her lips. 'I'm fine. Really. Just—just——'

'Last-minute nerves.' Marilyn smiled, too. 'Sure. I felt the same way.'

'Did you?' Hannah asked softly.

The other woman nodded and slipped her arm around Hannah's shoulders. 'I was scared stiff,' she said as they made their way slowly towards the door, 'and positive I was going to pass out the minute I heard the Bridal March begin.' She smiled. 'But then I saw Bob waiting at the altar, and all I could think about was that in just a little while we'd be husband and wife.' She gave Hannah a quick hug as they stepped into the hall. 'You just wait until you get yourself a look at that handsome brother of mine, honey. All your worries will fly away.'

But it didn't happen quite that way. If anything, that first glimpse of Grant, standing straight and tall at the far end of the room, only made Hannah's heart race even faster. He looked so forbidding, so remote and powerful. She wanted to turn and run away, to keep running and never come back.

But his eyes held her fast, those cool grey eyes; they locked on hers and seemed to draw her forward so that she walked slowly towards him while the strains of *Lohengrin* played softly on the grand piano in the sunroom. And then she was there, standing before him, her breathing quick and shallow.

Grant held out his hand.

'Hannah,' he said softly.

There was still time to run—but she lifted her chin and put her ice-cold hand in his. His fingers closed over hers, and the warmth of his touch surged through her. He drew her forward until she was standing close beside him, and then he smiled and something happened deep within her heart, something that was beyond description or comprehension, something that was dangerous and exciting, and all she could think of was that it was a damned good thing that theirs was going to be a celibate relationship.

It had been useless, arguing against a honeymoon.

'Is there somewhere special you'd like to go?' Grant had asked, and when she'd shaken her head he'd tossed off a list of possibilities as casually as if they were simply names on a shopping list. 'Spain? France? Italy? Perhaps something exotic. Japan—I've always wanted to see the Yasukuni Shrine.'

Hannah had listened with growing unease. Those places were all so far away, she'd thought. Her acquiescence to Grant's proposal, the wedding plans—all of that was unreal enough. Surely she'd feel even more estranged in such foreign surroundings?

'Or perhaps someplace warm,' he'd mused, when she hadn't answered. 'Mexico. The Caribbean.'

'Mexico,' she'd said quickly, automatically choosing the one that was closest to home. She'd never been there, but she knew people who had. Sally had returned from Acapulco with stories about crowds and music and days crammed with activities organised by the hotel social staff. It had sounded awful to Hannah, who much preferred being left to her own devices when she went on holiday. But this wasn't a holiday, it was a make-believe honeymoon with a man she barely knew. In those circumstances, days jammed with carefully arranged happenings sounded like a good idea.

'Fine,' he'd answered, and that had been the end of the discussion.

But as soon as their plane landed Hannah got the uneasy feeling that whatever lay ahead would not in any way resemble the vacations Sally or any of the other girls had described.

A long white limousine drove them to a sprawling series of pastel buildings tucked into a lush, tree-lined cove where an azure sea foamed whitely against a pale beach. A smiling bellman collected their luggage, then led them to a suite at least twice the size of Hannah's flat back in San Francisco. The sitting-room was exquisitely appointed, the bathroom was a wonder of black and rose marble, the bedroom—the bedroom was like something out of a fairy-tale, all white organdie, pale blue eyelet cotton, and tropical flowers. It was the kind of room women dreamed about, the sort you saw in perfume ads. All it lacked was a centrepiece, a pair of lovers locked in each other's arms.

'Well? What do you think?'

She turned quickly. Grant was standing in the doorway of the bedroom, watching her, his eyes unreadable behind dark aviator lenses, his hands tucked into the pockets of his casual chino trousers.

Her heart gave a funny little lurch. 'I—I think it's lovely,' she said. 'Where did you ever find it?'

He smiled. 'The travel agent recommended it. He said it was the perfect honeymoon spot.'

Hannah swung away from him. The perfect honeymoon spot. Yes, she supposed you'd certainly call it that—and as removed from the sort of place Sally had visited as day was from night. You didn't need to be a genius to figure out that there wouldn't be an organised activity in sight, just that impossibly blue ocean and long, deserted stretches of white sand, perfect for a bare handful of couples who would have eyes only for each other.

Why would Grant have chosen such a place? There was surely a limit to how far they had to play this little drama, especially now that they were safely out of sight of the people they knew. Being at a place such as this was only going to embarrass them. They wouldn't share any activities. Grant had already asked her if she knew how to scuba-dive and she'd told him she didn't.

'You don't know what you're missing,' he'd said, with a smile.

Perhaps. But he could dive all he wished, while she found a shady spot under a palm tree and read the handful of paperback books she'd brought with her. In the confines of a large, busy hotel, such behaviour would probably have gone unnoticed. But here, in the midst of all this togetherness, the two of them would stand out like—like mismatched linen on the oversized bed that dominated the bedroom of the suite.

'Shall I draw the bed curtains back, sir?' the bellman had asked with a little smile, as if he had seen hundreds of honeymoon couples and knew where they would be the moment he left them alone.

But not them. Not she and Grant. A little knot tightened within Hannah's breast.

'Hannah? Do you like it?'

She blinked and looked at Grant again. Why didn't he take off those glasses? It was unnerving, not being able to see his eyes.

She gave him a quick smile. 'It's—it's very pretty.'

Grant grinned. 'Very pretty? I think the management would kill itself if it heard you use such a tepid phrase to describe Paradise.'

Her smile was more genuine this time. 'Paradise?'

'*Paraiso*. Paradise. That's what it says on the towels.' He laughed as he leaned away from the door and strolled towards the built-in bar on the far side of the room. 'Don't look at me that way—I didn't pick the name.'

'No. Only the place.'

'Yes,' he said, as if he didn't hear the sharpness in her tone, 'I'll take the credit for that.' He whistled softly as he took a bottle of champagne from its ice bucket. 'Dom Perignon,' he said, 'and a vintage year. Very nice.'

'What made you choose this place, Grant?'

He nodded his head towards the windows. 'Take your pick. "Dazzling white beaches, water the colour of the sky..."' The cork popped softly and golden wine foamed lightly over the bottle top. 'Just what the travel agent promised.'

'And very much off the beaten track.'

'That, too.' He poured champagne into two crystal flutes, then held one out to her. 'A newly-weds' hideaway.'

Their eyes met, and something in the way he looked at her made Hannah flush.

'I—I don't think I want any wine, thank you.'

'Don't be silly. This is our honeymoon.' She looked at him, caught by a sudden tension in his voice, but she could tell nothing from the little she could see of his face. 'Go on,' he said, more gently, 'it'll relax you. You look all keyed up.'

Hannah hesitated, then reached for the glass. 'I'm just tired. It was a long flight.'

'And a long day.'

'Yes,' she admitted. 'It was.'

Grant sighed as he pulled off his sunglasses and tossed them on the bar.

'Marilyn went a little overboard, I guess.' He took a sip of his wine. When he spoke again, his voice sounded gruff. 'Was today anything like your first wedding?'

'No,' she said, 'it wasn't.'

'Ah,' he said. 'You went the whole route then. White gown, church, bridesmaids...'

Hannah shook her head as she thought back to that impetuous teenage marriage performed at City Hall.

'Actually,' she said softly, 'this was much nicer. Having the ceremony at home, with your family there...' She cleared her throat. 'And you? What was your wedding like?'

Grant smiled. 'My ex believed in extravaganzas,' he said. 'We had everything but dancing girls, and I think the only reason she didn't include them was because she was afraid they might steal her thunder.' He took a swallow of champagne. 'To tell you the truth, I think it's all overrated. It seems to me that what we did this time is a hell of a lot more honest.'

Hannah's smile faded. So much for making small talk, she thought. Sooner or later they would always get back to the reason they were together, not only for the next week but for the duration of their agreement, she and this man who was her husband, this—this stranger.

She felt a sudden jolt of despair. Why had she let him insist on this travesty of a honeymoon? It was bad enough she'd let him back her into this marriage, but——

'Hannah.' She looked up. Grant was watching her with a quiet intensity. 'You think I should have picked someplace less private, don't you?'

She flushed. 'I think it would have been easier, yes.'

He smiled slightly. 'Who knows? You may enjoy the next week more than you expect. Maybe we'll each take home some pleasant memories.'

His words sent an unexpected stab of pain into her heart. The reaction troubled her, and she dealt with it the only way she could, by beating a quick retreat to the safety of reality.

'It doesn't really matter, does it?' she said steadily. 'I mean, this isn't a real honeymoon, Grant, and we both know it, no matter what the rest of the world thinks.'

'Yes.' His smile was gone, as swiftly as if it had been wiped from his face. He scowled and tossed off the rest of his wine, then refilled his glass. 'And I suppose, sooner or later, we might as well get down to basics.'

Basics. Yes, of course. They'd never really had the chance to talk about what would have to be done: the selection of a doctor, all the technical details the magazine articles glossed over. That was what this was all about, wasn't it? Having a baby. It wasn't the usual way, but neither of them wanted that.

Hannah drew in her breath, then expelled it. 'Yes, we probably should get down to basics. I—I meant to ask you, in San Francisco...' Their eyes met, and a flush rose in her cheeks. 'Do you—do you know how to do it?'

Grant's brows lifted. 'How to do what?'

'The—the procedure,' she said stiffly. 'What will be required when——' She broke off in mid-sentence and her flush deepened. 'You know what I mean.'

'I'm afraid I don't, Hannah. I'm not very good at mind-reading.'

He looked puzzled and sounded innocent, damn him, but he was making fun of her! She knew it, just as he knew that talking about this part of their agreement embarrassed her.

'Well? Are you going to tell me what you're talking about, or am I supposed to guess?'

She took a deep breath.

'The baby,' she said calmly. 'I know a little about how we go about it, but not very much. I wondered if you——' Her flush deepened. 'I don't see what's so amusing, Grant,' she said stiffly. 'It's a perfectly reasonable question.'

'Cute,' he said softly. 'Very cute. I have to admit, I wouldn't have pegged you for playing games, Hannah, but hell, if that's what you want to do——'

'Cute? What's cute?' Her eyes widened as he put down his glass, then took hers and put it down, too. 'What are you doing?'

'I thought it might take me a while to get you into the mood, but...' He smiled as he took her into his arms. 'I've always believed in accommodating a woman's wishes.'

Hannah stared at him. 'Grant?' A rill of panic threaded her voice as he gathered her closer. 'Grant, stop!'

'Actually,' he said softly, 'I've been negligent, darling.' His hands spread on her shoulders. 'Here we are, husband and wife, and I've yet to kiss you.'

'You did,' she said quickly. 'After the judge pronounced us——'

'That wasn't a kiss, Hannah, it was a formality.' His breath warmed her cheek as he bent his head. 'Let me show you what a kiss should be,' he said, and his mouth descended on hers.

She made a murmur of distress and turned away from him. 'What are you doing?'

He clasped her face in his hands. 'No more games,' he said huskily. 'Not now.'

Hannah's throat constricted. 'I don't know what you're talking about, Grant. Please——'

His mouth was cool and soft as it silenced her, moving with slow assurance against her lips. She struggled and he moved back, taking her with him, until he was leaning against the wall and she was gathered closely in his arms.

'Grant,' she said, 'don't.'

'Kiss me,' he whispered. His tongue slid along the seam of her lips. 'It's all right now, Hannah, you can let go. It's all right, darling.'

She could feel the heavy beat of his heart against hers, feel the heat of his body. He was warm, like the sun blazing down on the white sand, and he smelled like the sea, clean and salty and powerful. Her heartbeat quickened, then began to pound. She felt as she had in that one dizzying instant when he had taken her hand and drawn her forward to the altar hours ago; she felt as if she were melting, as if she might fall to the floor in a boneless heap unless she had the steadying support of Grant's arms...

'You're not made of ice,' he whispered, 'no matter how you try to pretend.' He bit gently at her lip. 'Open to me, Hannah, let me taste you.'

'No. Grant, no. You can't!'

'I can, damn you,' he said with a rough passion. 'You're my wife!'

His wife. His wife.

The words beat through her, sang in her blood, and she swayed in her arms as he gathered her even closer to him, holding her so tightly that she could no longer tell where her body ended and his began.

'You're so beautiful,' he whispered. His hands threaded into her hair and he tilted her face up to his. 'I love the way you look when I touch you, Hannah. Your eyes get all smoky, your mouth turns soft...'

'Grant,' she said in a breathless whisper, 'Grant, listen to me. We can't—I don't want——'

She caught her breath on a long-drawn-out sob as he bit lightly at her neck. Her head fell back and he whispered her name as he kissed her throat.

'Yes, you do,' he said thickly. He caught her mouth with his. His tongue slipped between her lips again and she gave a moan of pleasure. 'You want this,' he said, and he slid his hands down her body, his thumbs just brushing her breasts before they settled at her waist. 'And this.' He caught her and lifted her against him, so that her loins were cradled against the hard arousal of his flesh.

'Grant,' she said frantically, 'Grant——'

'That's what you do to me,' he said in a soft, urgent whisper. He took her hand and brought it between them. 'Do you feel that, Hannah? It's for you, darling, all for you.'

She whimpered as he gathered her into the curve of one arm and traced the outline of her body with his fingertips, then cupped her breast. His thumb moved, and she felt her nipple spring erect to seek his touch.

'Oh,' she whispered, 'oh...'

Stop him, she told herself, stop him now, before it's too late. Stop him before this goes too far and there's no turning back.

His fingers were at her throat, opening the buttons that ran down the front of her dress.

'Beautiful,' he said softly, when he finally eased the pink silk off her shoulders. He bent his head and kissed the swell of each breast rising above her white lace teddy, and a tremor of almost unbearable excitement went through her. 'Now it's your turn,' he said, and he drew her hands to his shirt.

No, she thought, no, I won't do it. But her fingers were already skimming lightly down the soft cotton, trembling as they undid the buttons, and then she tugged the shirt free of his trousers and slipped it back on his shoulders.

'Touch me,' he said, and she put her palms flat against his chest, closing her eyes as she felt the silken kiss of the dark, lightly curling hair, the warm heat of his muscled skin.

'I knew it would be like this,' he said fiercely, and the words raced through her blood.

Yes, oh, yes, she had known it, too. She had always known it. She'd wanted him from the beginning; what was the sense of denying it? And he wanted her, she knew that, she'd known it all along. All the talk of contracts and babies was only window-dressing.

This—the magic, the flashfire that was always waiting to blaze into life, that had always threatened to overwhelm them—this was the only thing that meant anything. Her breath caught as Grant kissed her deeply. Desire, thick and hot, moved through her veins.

He groaned softly as she touched him, as she discovered the long, hard lines of muscle in his back and shoulders. Liquid heat built low in her belly. This was reality, and, if she had been foolish enough to think she could live with Grant without giving in to it, her only comfort was that he had been the same kind of fool.

Her head fell back as he swung her up into his arms and carried her through the sitting-room to the bedroom beyond, and he captured the sound of her surrender in his mouth, returned it to her in the whisper of her own name and the heat of his breath as he kissed her. He let her down beside the bed slowly, so that her breasts brushed his chest, her belly grazed his, and he drew back the curtains. Then he gathered her to him again and kissed her, over and over, as if he could never get enough of her mouth. She reached up and clung to his wrists as his hands cupped her face, drinking from his mouth as he drank from hers.

'Tell me you want me,' he said.

His face was almost lost in shadow, but she could see his eyes, glittering with desire. You can still stop, a little voice within her whispered urgently; there's time.

But his mouth fell on hers again, and when he lifted his head she was beyond reason, beyond anything but the wildness building with each tick of her heart.

'Yes,' she said in a low voice. 'Oh, yes, Grant. I do. I always have.'

He laughed softly and triumphantly as he shrugged free of his shirt. With deft fingers, he undid the rest of her dress and it fell to the floor like the petals of a pink rose.

'We're going to be incredible together,' he said softly. 'I knew that from the first time I touched you.'

A smile trembled on her lips. 'Did you?' she whispered, cupping his face in her hands as he had cupped hers, letting her thumbs follow the curve of his high cheekbones, letting her fingertips learn the sweet, hard lines of his mouth while his hands curled around her hips.

He caught her finger between his teeth and sucked on it, then bit lightly on the soft pad of flesh below her thumb.

'Yes.' He pressed his open mouth over her breast and she cried out softly as his teeth closed lightly on the hardened nub of flesh rising just beneath the white lace of her teddy. 'After I left you that first night, I almost came back.'

Hannah smiled and buried her face against his throat. 'I wouldn't have let you in.'

'I'd have kicked down your door and taken you anyway,' he said huskily.

She felt herself quickening at his whispered words. 'I'd have fought you.'

Grant laughed. 'Not for long.'

Colour stained her cheeks. 'Why didn't you?' she whispered. 'Why did you wait all this time?'

'I don't know.' He drew her to him. 'Maybe because I was never sure if I wanted to kiss you or kill you,' he said with a little laugh as he bore her down into the soft depths of the bed.

'And now you are?'

'Yes.' He drew down the strap of her teddy and kissed the flesh beneath. 'Why would I want to do anything but make love to you, now that I've got you sweet and warm in my bed?' He gave her a long, slow kiss. 'I wondered, Will she give herself to me because she wants to, or will she be a cold stone performing the terms of the contract?'

Hannah's smile faltered. 'What?'

Grant ran his hand the length of her body. 'I have my answer now, don't I, sweet?' He bent and kissed her mouth. 'Yes,' he murmured, 'oh, yes.'

'Grant?' Hannah struggled back against the pillows.

'Don't talk now.' He growled softly as he nipped at her throat. 'Give me your hand,' he whispered, 'and——'

'No. Grant, please.' She pushed at his shoulders, and he went still. 'What did you mean about—about me being a cold stone performing the terms of—of the contract?'

He rolled to his side and looked down at her. 'What?' He gave an exasperated little laugh. 'Hell, I wasn't taking notes.'

She sat up, suddenly painfully aware of how abandoned she must look in nothing more substantial than a white lace teddy, with her hair tumbling around her shoulders and her lipstick smeared, and she reached for the bedspread and tried, as best she could, to drag it to her chin.

'What did you mean?' she insisted.

'Hannah——'

She drew in her breath. 'The contract doesn't give you the right to—to take me to bed, and you know it.'

'My God, woman.' He gave a relieved laugh. 'Are we going to have a discussion of legal niceties here? OK. Technically, I suppose you have a point.' He reached out and caught her wrist. 'Our marriage licence does that. Now, come over here, and——'

Hannah slapped his hand away. 'I don't know what you're talking about, Grant. Nothing gives you the right to—to——'

'What's the problem here, Hannah?' he said, his voice suddenly cold and flat.

She stared at him. 'The problem? The problem,' she said, her voice shaking, 'is that you seem to think you had the right to—to do what you were just doing.'

'What I was doing,' he said, his eyes locked on her face, 'was making love to my wife.'

'You mean, you were trying to seduce me.'

His brow furrowed. 'Forgive me,' he said in a soft, dangerous voice, 'but I don't quite see the distinction.'

Hannah gathered the bedspread more closely around herself. 'We agreed there'd be no—no sex between us, but you——'

'What the *hell* are you babbling about?' Grant rolled to the edge of the mattress, got to his feet, and slapped his hands on his hips. 'How did you expect to have this baby, Hannah? By going out to look in a cabbage patch, or waiting for the stork to drop one into your lap?'

Her face coloured. 'The way we agreed, of course. Artificial insemination, Grant. We said——'

The rude, harsh sound of his laughter roared through the rooms. She felt a flush of shameful colour rise under her skin and flood her face as he laughed and laughed.

'Let me get this straight,' he gasped. 'You thought—you really thought—that I'd agreed to—to make love to a test-tube?'

'Yes.' Angry tears rose in her eyes. 'Yes, of course. That's what you said. That's what we discussed. We——'

His laughter became a snarl of rage, and Hannah cried out as he grabbed hold of her and dragged her across the bed.

'You thought I'd agree to put a ring on your finger, give you my name—hell, give you my child—and do it all without ever touching you?' he said through clenched teeth.

Hannah grimaced as she tried to wrench free. 'That was our deal.'

'No.' His lips drew back from his teeth. 'No, Hannah, it was not our deal. What kind of woman are you?'

'Not the kind who sleeps with a man because she's—she's signed a scrap of paper!'

Grant's face twisted with fury. 'You make that sound like a morality lesson. But what kind of morality is it that makes you think it's better to conceive a child in a test-tube rather than in a man's arms?'

'That was your idea, not mine. You're the one who proposed it!'

He grabbed her shoulder as she started to turn away. 'No, I did not! What did you plan on telling our child when it was old enough? That it was conceived in a glass dish?'

Hannah swung her feet to the floor. 'Get out,' she said in a trembling voice. 'Do you hear me, Grant? Get out of this room!'

'With pleasure.' He stalked to the door, then swung around and faced her. 'Tomorrow——'

'Tomorrow, you can start the annulment proceedings.'

'No.'

'Why not? You're the attorney, not I.'

'No annulment.' His nostrils flared. 'And no divorce. Not until you've conceived my child.'

She stared at him in disbelief. 'You can't be serious.'

A cold smile angled across his mouth. 'No?'

'You can't hold me to—to a piece of paper that says that——'

'Try me.'

'Don't be ridiculous,' she whispered, her eyes riveted to his stony face.

'You've agreed to stay married to me until we conceive a child—or until our agreement expires.'

'But that's—that's three years,' she said desperately. 'No court would—would hold me to such a thing.'

Grant's eyes narrowed. 'Perhaps not.'

'Well, then——'

'Get a lawyer and challenge the agreement, if you don't like it.'

'I couldn't afford the cost of——'

'No. You couldn't.' He smiled unpleasantly. 'Especially when you add the risk of me winning the countersuit for punitive damages and costs.'

'What damages? What costs?'

'The emerald on your finger. Every piece of clothing in those very expensive pieces of luggage. The mental cruelty I'll have suffered because of your breach of contract.' He smiled. 'I can be a very convincing victim, Hannah, a wealthy, successful man who wanted an heir and was duped by a beautiful woman into signing an agreement——'

'No one would believe that,' she said, her voice shaking.

'—an agreement she now refuses to honour.' He laughed softly. 'Hell, think of the legal ground we'd break! The case could take years.' His smile vanished in the blink of an eye. 'And could cost millions.'

'You bastard!' Hannah had gone white. 'You know I can't——'

His smile was smug. 'Then you're stuck, aren't you, darling?'

'I'll—I'll tell everyone about you,' she said, her voice rising. 'I'll tell them what kind of man you are, that you're blackmailing me——'

'Try it—if you can get anybody to listen. My guess is that they'll be too busy laughing.'

'They'll laugh at you, too, Grant. Have you thought of that?'

'Ah, but that's the difference between us, sweetheart.' His mouth twisted. 'I don't give a damn what anybody thinks of me, remember?'

She stared at him in horror as he walked slowly, almost insolently, to the bedroom door, and then she shrieked his name and flew after him.

'You can't do this!'

He turned and pulled her into his arms. 'There's only one way out of this,' he said roughly, and he kissed her, not with passion but with rage. When he was finished, he flung her from him so that she fell back against the wall. 'Think it over. When you reach a decision, I'll be waiting.'

'Never,' she screamed as he strode into the sitting-room. 'Do you hear me, Grant? Never!' She reached out and slammed the door shut. 'Never,' she whispered, and then she threw herself on the bed, rolled on to her belly, and sobbed her heart out.

CHAPTER NINE

NIGHT came at last, and Hannah fell into an exhausted sleep, never stirring until morning when the freshening wind snatched at the bedroom shutter and slammed it against the window-frame.

'Grant?' she said, scrambling up against the pillows.

Her whisper was greeted by a silence that was only broken by the pounding beat of her heart. A quick glance assured her that the door between the sitting-room and bedroom was still closed. After a moment, she threw aside the blanket, pulled on her robe, and padded to the balcony.

The breeze, fragrant with the scent of the sea, blew her hair back from her face as she opened the door and stepped outside. Hannah sank down into a wicker rocker, tucked her feet up beneath her, and laid her head back.

How beautiful this place was. The sun was a golden disc in the blue sky; the beat of the sea was like the whisper of the planet's heart.

Paradise, Grant had called it. Yes. That was what it would seem to the other honeymooning guests who slept safe in each other's arms. Hannah smiled bitterly. It was a pretty safe bet that no other couple in the hotel had spent the night as she and her groom had, lying cold and apart, separated not just by a wall but by an anger so great it bordered on hate.

Hannah shuddered. A few short weeks ago she'd been content with her life. If it had no emotional highs, neither did it have any terrible lows. She'd had a good job, an apartment of her own—things that might not seem like much but were more than enough to satisfy her needs.

Now—now she had nothing. No job, no home, certainly not the warm, sweet future she'd let Grant convince her lay ahead.

She choked. No. That wasn't quite accurate. She had something, all right, she had Grant's wedding-band on her finger and his promise—his threat—that he would not let her go until she had lived up to their agreement.

And she would never do that. Never.

She dropped one bare foot to the floor and set the rocker in motion. How could he ever have thought she'd agreed to the sort of marriage he'd described? Only a woman with no self-respect would go to a man's bed night after night knowing that he wanted her for no other reason than to fulfil the terms of an impossible contract, knowing that he felt nothing for her except his need for a woman's body.

Not that she wanted him to have feelings for her. Hannah stood up and padded softly to the balcony railing. She certainly had none for him, unless you counted the insane sexual need for him whenever he touched her, and last night's ugly scene had eliminated that forever.

She would never let him touch her again—and, as soon as he realised that, he would surely agree to put an end to this farce of a marriage.

The soft breeze blew a strand of hair across Hannah's face, and she tucked it behind her ear. It wouldn't even be a matter of getting him to agree. He'd had plenty of time to calm down by now. He was a rational man, logical by training and by instinct; he had to have reached the same conclusions she had. He had to know they had no choice but to fly back to the States and end things as discreetly and quickly as possible.

She would even accept some of the blame herself, instead of laying it all on him.

'We misunderstood each other, Grant,' she said softly, as if he were standing before her, 'but it's not the end of the world. I'm willing to admit we made a mistake, and I'm certain you are, too.'

With a little nod of self-assurance, Hannah strode into the bedroom and prepared to face him.

She showered, pulled on a bright print dress and a pair of leather sandals, then sat before the dressing-table and put on just enough make-up to put colour into her cheeks. She had seen Grant negotiate; he would see a woebegone look as a sign of weakness, and she could not afford to seem weak in this encounter. Grant was too strong and formidable an opponent for that. Wasn't that why she was in this mess in the first place, because she'd let him roll over her objections to marrying him?

She applied a light coating of mascara to her dark lashes, then stroked a warm coral lipstick over her mouth. She brushed her hair until it crackled with electricity, then hesitated. Glasses? Or contact lenses? The glasses lent a more authoritative look, she decided, and she plopped them on her nose.

Her courage almost failed her when she reached for the doorknob. She pressed her ear to the door, but she could hear nothing. Was he still asleep? Or—or was he gone? Hope surged in her heart. Maybe he'd not only reached the same conclusions she'd reached, maybe he'd acted upon them.

Well, there was only one way to find out. Hannah smoothed down her skirt, squared her shoulders, and flung the door open.

He was there, all right, standing at the bay window on the far side of the room, sipping what looked like orange juice as he stared out to sea—and he was naked.

No. Hannah's heart thudded against her ribs. Not naked, exactly. He was wearing a towel draped around his hips. Her gaze flew over him. He must have been swimming: water glistened on his tanned shoulders, glinted like tiny crystals in his dark hair.

Once, on a quiet Sunday spent in a small museum, she'd rounded a corner and come upon a Greek statue in a sunlit alcove, a life-size figure of a man so perfect, so beautiful, that the sight had sent something that was almost a pain knifing into her heart.

It was the way she felt now, looking at Grant. He was standing absolutely still, caught in a ray of soft morning sunlight so that his skin looked golden. The statue had been marble, cold even to look at, but Grant's flesh would be warm, warmer now than it had been last night, when her fingers had drifted over those muscled shoulders, the hard, clefted back, when she'd felt the satiny brush of his skin against her naked breasts...

She started to turn away, but it was too late. Grant swung towards her. Something glinted in his eyes—surprise, perhaps—and then his face became closed.

'Good morning.'

His tone was unreadable but the greeting was civilised. It was, at least, a start. Hannah took a breath.

'Good morning,' she said.

'Did you sleep well?'

Was that sarcasm? She looked at him, saw nothing in the cool grey eyes, and decided that, even if that had been a gauntlet tossed down, she'd feign ignorance of having noticed.

'Very well,' she answered.

'I'm glad one of us did.' He smiled pleasantly. 'That sofa's not as comfortable as it looks.'

Hannah's eyes narrowed. That had to have been a barb. But he was still smiling politely, as if a discussion of sleeping habits were one they had all the time, as if the night just passed had not been the first of their marriage...

As if he were not standing there wearing little more than that damned smile.

'Would you like some fresh orange juice? Or coffee? The porter delivered a tray a few minutes ago.'

Either one would stick in her throat. But either was preferable to just standing here, with nothing but Grant to look at.

'Coffee would be fine,' she said with a quick smile. 'Where did he put——?'

'Over there. No, don't bother, I'll get it.' He smiled back at her. 'I want some more juice, anyway.'

He walked towards her slowly. She could see the flex of muscle beneath his skin. Her gaze flew to his chest, where drops of water glittered in the dark, silken hair, then fell lower to where the hair arrowed down his flat belly and disappeared beneath the towel so casually knotted across his hips.

'How do you want it, Hannah?' His voice was soft, a little husky. She looked up quickly, and their eyes met.

'How do I want what?' she whispered.

He smiled lazily. 'Your coffee. Do you want cream and sugar?'

She let out her breath. 'Oh. Oh, no, I—I take it black.'

Grant poured the coffee and handed it to her. 'It's funny, isn't it?' he said. 'My having to ask you a question like that, I mean. You know how I take my coffee, whether I like mayonnaise or mustard on my ham sandwich, you probably even know what size shirt I wear—and yet I know very little about you.'

Hannah took a swallow of coffee. It was hot and very strong. Maybe it would clear the cobwebs from her head, because if this conversation had a direction she had yet to discern it.

'I guess that's right,' she said.

'Why is that, do you think?'

She looked at him. There was an expression that could best be defined as interest on his face. Was this more polite chit-chat—or was he manoeuvring her again, in some way she could not understand?

'Well,' she said, after a few seconds, 'that's not unusual. That's usually how it is with secretaries and employers.'

Grant nodded. 'I suppose. But then, you're not my secretary.'

He smiled pleasantly, and she did, too, even though she felt as if she were two people, one standing here having this impersonal conversation with a half-naked man who had only hours ago told her she had no choice but to give herself to him, the other trying desperately to figure out what the hell was going on.

Was he trying to make amends for his behaviour last night? Was he telling her that he knew they'd made a mistake?

Hannah smiled, too. 'Well, no,' she said, 'I'm not your secretary, I'm your paralegal, but it comes down to the same——'

'You're not my paralegal either.' His smile tilted just a bit. 'Not any more. As of yesterday afternoon, you became my wife——'

Their eyes met, and what she saw in his made the cup tremble in her hand. She turned and put both cup and saucer down on the table.

'—or have you managed to put that unpleasant detail out of your head?'

She looked up at him. He was still smiling, but now his smile looked as if it had been painted on.

'Grant——'

'I doubt if a newly-wed couple has ever used this suite as poorly as we've used it,' he said.

'Grant, listen——'

'That bed wasn't made for one.' He stepped closer to her, so close that she could smell the faint salty tang of the sea on his body. 'You looked very small and alone in it last night.'

Her eyes flew to his. 'When did you——?'

'You needn't look so alarmed. I didn't lay a hand on you.' His mouth twisted. 'Hell, if I were into force, I'd have used it yesterday instead of taking a ten-mile run on the beach.'

'I don't under——'

'I'm talking about working off frustration.' He smiled tightly. 'Cold showers work too, but you, my lovely wife, had pre-empted access to the shower.'

Hannah felt her cheeks redden, but when she spoke her voice was calm.

'About—about being your wife.' She took a deep breath. 'We have to talk about that,' she said. 'I can't be. Surely you know that now.'

He looked at her for a long moment, and then he reached out and stroked the hair back from her flushed face, the gesture curiously gentle and at odds with the dark look in his eyes.

His answer was a monotone. 'Yes.'

Hannah's heart lifted. 'I was sure you'd understand,' she said quickly. 'I just knew——'

'And we will talk, over breakfast. Just give me a minute to change, and I'll join you.'

It was over, then, she thought as she stood near the window in the sitting-room and waited for him. Soon, all this would be finished.

Good. That was what she wanted, to put this behind her so that in time she wouldn't remember any of it. She would forget everything. The way Grant had looked at her when she'd come down the aisle towards him; the way he'd taken her in his arms once they were alone; the way her body sang under the magic of his kisses and his hands.

'Hannah?'

She sprang to her feet as the bedroom door opened. Grant was standing there, smiling, dressed in white canvas jeans and a navy blue T-shirt, and, when she saw him, something happened deep within her heart, something so fierce and unexpected that it sent a shudder racing through her.

'Hannah? Are you all right?'

She nodded. 'Yes. I—I'm fine. I just—I think I need some air.'

'Let's take a walk along the beach,' he said, and somehow she managed to smile her agreement, even take his hand when he offered it to her.

'That sounds nice.'

They strolled slowly along the shoreline, close together like the few other couples they saw, and Hannah knew they must look as if they, too, had created a little world all their own, but it was the worst kind of lie. While the other couples were whispering words of love, Grant was talking very quietly about his errors of judgement.

'I wouldn't have suggested it if I hadn't thought it would work,' he said. 'I want you to understand that, Hannah.'

She nodded. 'I do. And I want you to understand that—that I know I'm not blameless.'

He shook his head. 'That's kind of you, but it's not true. You tried to tell me this wouldn't work, right from the start.'

'I mean——' She hesitated. 'I mean,' she said, clearing her throat, 'it was foolish of me to assume you'd—you'd agreed to a marriage of convenience. Thinking back, it seems impossible that I could have been so stupid.'

Grant shrugged his shoulders. 'That was no crazier than my ideas.'

'I'm just glad you understand. I was afraid you might not see it my way, that you might—you might insist we—we——'

'No.' He laughed sharply. 'No, I may be a lot of things, but I'm not a man who believes in forcing a woman into his bed.'

'Then you agree—our situation is impossible.'

He nodded. 'It is.'

Hannah let out her breath. There it was, out in the open. She'd been right, then. Grant was not only calmer this morning, he was back to being the practical, self-disciplined man he'd always been. Their marriage, such as it was, was finished. Relief, tinged by a bitter-sweet emotion, flooded through her.

'I'm glad we don't have to quarrel about it,' she said. 'I thought you'd see it this way, I hoped you would, but——'

'I've already arranged to check out of the hotel. And I've arranged for a car to be delivered to us at ten.'

'Ten? That's not very much time, is it? We'd better start to pack.'

Grant put his arm around her as she started to turn back towards the hotel.

'The chambermaid's taking care of that.'

Hannah let out her breath as they began walking again. 'Then—then I guess all that's left is deciding what we'll tell everyone back home.'

'Not to worry.'

She looked at him in surprise. 'What do you mean?'

'I phoned Marilyn early this morning, and I cabled the office.' His arm tightened around her. 'Everything's all taken care of, darling.'

'But—what did you tell them?' She looked up at him. 'I thought about that—about what we could say to everyone—and—and I couldn't come up with anything.'

Grant smiled. 'If practising law has taught me one valuable lesson,' he said, 'it's that there's nothing wrong in giving a truthful answer if the truth fits the situation.'

Hannah looked at him again. Why did she have this strange feeling that they were talking about two different things?

'Well, yes,' she said slowly, 'but considering the circumstances...' She ran the tip of her tongue along her lips. 'You couldn't—you didn't—we can't very well tell them the truth, Grant, not after what we told them about why we were getting married so quickly.'

'That we'd fallen head over heels in love, you mean?'

She nodded. How shabby the lie sounded now.

'Exactly,' she said. 'So what could you have said that would possibly——?'

'I told you, darling. The truth.'

Hannah came to a stop and swung to face him. 'You keep saying that as if it's a code word or something, but I've no idea what you're talking about.'

'I told them that falling madly in love is wonderful——'

'What?'

'—so wonderful, in fact, that we've decided we can't possibly make do with a one-week honeymoon.'

She felt the blood drain from her face. 'What are you saying?'

'It's simple. I made a mistake, thinking you'd be ready to consummate our marriage immediately.'

She gaped at him. His face bore a cool, calm look, one that she had seen before, and it sent a chill through her, for it said, more clearly than words ever could, that the disagreement between them was far from over.

'You mean, you made a mistake thinking I'd consummate it at all,' she said, her eyes locked on his.

Grant shook his head. 'I meant exactly what I said.' His voice was low-pitched and filled with assurance. 'We really don't know each other. Oh, we've worked together for several months——'

'Five,' Hannah said stupidly. 'Five months, that's all.'

'Right. Five months. And for most of that time we barely looked at each other.' He slid his arm around her shoulders and they began walking again. 'You were Miss Lewis, I was Mr MacLean.'

'Grant.' She swallowed drily. 'I still don't follow you. We've already agreed, this was a mistake.'

'Yes. Trying to make love to you yesterday was a mistake,' he said bluntly. 'I've no excuse to offer, Hannah. Hell, I figured it was enough that we want to go to bed with each other; I——'

Hannah twisted out from his encircling arm. 'Speak for yourself,' she said tautly.

A slow smile tilted across his mouth. 'Don't lie to me or yourself,' he said softly.

'I don't lie! If you think I'm going to—to feed your monstrous ego by—by letting you say things that——'

He caught her in his arms and kissed her before she could finish the sentence, his mouth dropping to hers so hard and fast that she hadn't time to step back or even to turn her head away.

Hannah slammed her fists against his chest. 'Damn you,' she hissed. 'What do you think you're going to——?'

'Shut up, Hannah,' he said fiercely. 'Just shut the hell up and kiss me.'

His mouth was cool, much cooler than the sun blazing down overhead, but it flamed against hers, as hot as the stroke of his hands along her spine and across her hips.

'Kiss me,' he whispered again, and suddenly she was, kissing him over and over, her mouth open to the taste of his, her arms slipping up to curl around his neck and bring his head down to hers.

When they finally broke apart, her breathing was ragged. Grant looked at her for what seemed an eternity, and then he clasped her face in his hands.

'The house is on a mountain,' he said, his eyes on hers, 'a million miles from anywhere.'

Hannah's world was spinning. 'What—what house?'

Grant smiled. 'The one I've rented for us. I had to take it without seeing it, of course, but the agent who made the arrangements assured me that it's perfect for honeymooners.'

'Grant. Grant, please——'

'It comes staffed with a cook and a housekeeper. And it's very private, with a garden and a pool.' He smiled. 'But if we get tired of lazing around in the sun there are Mayan ruins not far away, and we can always drive to Cozumel or Cancun for entertainment.'

'My God, Grant, what have you done?'

He laughed softly. 'I'm trying to tell you, darling. I've rented a house for us for the rest of the month.'

Hannah's eyes widened in shock. 'Are you crazy? A house, for the month? But you said—you said you agreed, that our situation was impossible.'

'And it is. We certainly can't continue on the way we are. This marriage——'

'It isn't a marriage! We only entered into it to——'

'You don't have to remind me,' he growled. 'Believe me, Hannah, I know the reason for this union.'

She let out a breath. 'And—and you agreed when I said it had to end; you said——'

'And it will,' Grant said calmly. 'Once you've met the terms of our contract.'

She stared at him in disbelief. He had to be joking. He had to be! Surely he wasn't going to try and hold her to their ugly arrangement?

'It won't be that impossible, Hannah.' His hands slipped to her shoulders. 'After a few days, we won't be strangers to each other any more. You'll feel more at ease with me——'

'Is that all you think it will take to get me into your bed?' She gave a sharp laugh. 'I'm at ease with—with the man who does my dry-cleaning, but that doesn't mean I'd——'

'You're forgetting something.' His hands tightened on her until she could feel the bite of each finger in her flesh. 'No matter what lies you tell yourself, you know you want to make love with me.'

'It's not making love,' she said in a shaken, angry whisper, 'it's—it's having sex!'

His eyes darkened, and his voice was as hard as the hands holding her. 'Whatever you say.'

'That's what it is, isn't it?' She glared at him, her chin tilted at a proud angle. 'It's—it's sex for pay, nothing else.'

'Hannah!' A muscle jumped in Grant's jaw. 'Goddammit, I'm warning you!'

'I know you are. You've warned me. You'll force me to uphold my end of our agreement or ruin me.' The breath rasped in her throat. 'Well, you'll have to ruin me, then, Grant, because I've no intention of—of prostituting myself for you.'

Silence fell between them. Hannah was shaking inside, but she forced herself to meet Grant's furious glare without flinching. It seemed a long time before he lifted his hands from her shoulders with exaggerated care and gave her a cold smile.

'Believe me, your eagerness to end our relationship is matched only by my own. You have my assurance that I won't prolong things a day more than necessary.'

Hannah's chin lifted. 'I've no intention of staying married to you. You might as well get that through your head.'

'And you might as well remember what I told you last night. There'll be no divorce.'

'I'll leave you anyway, and don't bother reminding me that I have no job and no place to live——'

'And no way to get back to San Francisco unless I pay for your ticket.'

'That's not true.' Her heart was thudding so loudly she was afraid he could hear it. 'I have money of my own.'

'You have fifty dollars in your purse.' His smile was all teeth. 'I took the liberty of checking this morning. That won't get you very far, darling.'

She stared at him. 'I have credit cards.'

'Not any more.'

'You took them?' Her eyes widened in shock. 'You had no right!'

'I have every right. You're my wife.'

'You—you...' Her breath sputtered. 'You bastard! You son of a bitch! You—you——'

'Four weeks, Hannah.' His voice was calm, which only infuriated her more. 'That's hardly a lifetime.'

'No.' She drew in her breath as she stared into his eyes. 'But it's more than enough time for me to hate you as I've never hated another human being in my life!'

She turned and started back towards the hotel, when Grant reached out and caught hold of her.

'It doesn't have to be that way,' he said.

Hannah swung around. 'I should have known,' she said furiously. 'You can't bear not getting your own way, can you, Grant?' Her hands balled into fists. 'And you'll even keep me a prisoner to do it!'

Grant's mouth narrowed. 'You have it all wrong.' His hands slid down her arms until he was clasping her wrists. 'What I'm doing is keeping you my wife.'

Hannah stared at him in silence. He moved no nearer and made no attempt to draw her to him, but his nearness, and the memory of his touch, were enough.

She gave a muffled cry, wrenched herself free, and flew across the sand to the relative safety of the hotel.

CHAPTER TEN

How easy it was to control your world, if you were Grant MacLean. Hannah watched with cool detachment as everyone scurried to do his bidding.

Their luggage was packed and waiting in the lobby when they returned to the hotel; the bill was ready and presented discreetly for Grant's signature and at almost the same moment a gleaming black Land Rover pulled up outside the doors.

'Let's go,' Grant said briskly. His hand fastened around hers in a gesture that might look loving but was, in reality, a manacle.

Hannah's heart was racing, but she gave Grant a cool stare. Did he think she was going to make a scene? Well, she wasn't. She had no intention of letting him see how angry and frightened she was. She would, instead, retaliate in the only way she could, and treat his power with contempt.

'You don't need to handcuff me,' she said coldly.

She wrenched her hand from his, marched to the Land Rover, and threw the door open. Once inside, she sat unmoving while he supervised the loading of their luggage, her face a mask that slipped only when the head porter bade them goodbye.

'*Vaya con Dios*,' he said with a polite smile.

Hannah had to bite back the urge to tell him she was going not with God but with the devil.

They made good time along the main road. Signs flashed by for the *aeropuerto* and Hannah had one instant of almost breathless hope that everything he'd said had been nothing but angry words said to upset her, but the signs were quickly behind them and they were heading up a narrow road that climbed into the mountains.

They passed through a town, then through little villages. She kept waiting for Grant to slow the car and turn into one of them, but he kept his foot firmly on the accelerator. The road narrowed again, until it was only a dirt track, and still they climbed.

Maybe he hadn't been exaggerating when he'd said he was taking her a million miles from anywhere. But why? What was he planning?

She glanced at him cautiously, taking in the harsh profile, the narrowed mouth and jutting jaw. What had he said about his reasons for staying on in Mexico for the month? 'We don't really know each other.' Did he really think that in four short weeks they *would* come to know each other? Did he think all it would take to get her into his bed was knowing that he liked dogs and helped little old ladies across the street?

Hannah clasped her hands in her lap. She knew everything she needed to know about Grant MacLean. Grant MacLean got what he wanted, or else.

That was what this was all about. She'd resisted his sexual advances...

No. That was a lie.

She shifted uneasily in her seat. She *had* responded to him; there was no point in pretending she hadn't. But the fever in her blood had turned to ice once she'd understood what his intentions were.

She'd thought he'd been as swept up in passion as she, but the truth was that her seduction had been nothing more than a detail of their arrangement. Sally had been quite right: Grant had no heart, he had only an ego a mile wide.

She could not imagine ever feeling desire for him again, much less passion. The house he'd rented had eight rooms, he'd said. Hannah blew out her breath. Fine. She would avoid him. When he was in the kitchen, she'd be in the bathroom. When he was outside, she'd be inside. And whatever bedroom she chose would be as far from his as possible.

Would he endure four weeks of that? She gave him another tight-lipped glance. No, she didn't think so. A week would probably be more than enough. By then, even Grant would be willing to admit failure. They would fly home, and he'd have to endure the raised eyebrows and speculative whispers that would surely greet the announcement that their whirlwind courtship had led straight to a whirlwind divorce.

'I don't give a damn what people think,' he'd said, but it wasn't true. He cared what people thought as much as anybody. More, perhaps, considering the size of his damned ego.

'If the directions the agent gave us are accurate, we should be there soon.'

She looked up. Grant was concentrating on the road ahead, his hands lying lightly on the steering-wheel. His tone was conversational.

Hannah almost laughed. She hoped he enjoyed talking to himself.

'And just take a look at that view. Damn, but it's spectacular.'

The man sounded just like a tourist. Her chin lifted. If he thought some pleasant chit-chat was going to change anything, he was——

'—crazy.' She swung towards him, and he flashed a quick smile. 'Hell, I must have been, agreeing to rent a house sight unseen, then finding out it's ten thousand feet straight up a mountainside.'

Ten thousand feet? Surely he wasn't serious?

'Well, the agent swore the trip's worth it.' The engine hummed as he downshifted on the steepening grade. 'He says the forest comes right up to the back door. And the view goes on forever. He says...' Grant glanced past her and gave a long, slow whistle. 'Wow!' he whispered.

Wow? Hannah's jaw clenched. What did 'wow' mean?

'Forever is right,' he murmured. He chuckled softly. 'I just hope this car has good brakes.'

He was trying to get a reaction from her. Well, she wasn't about to oblige. Still, she couldn't resist taking one swift peek out of the corner of her eye.

'Oh, God.' She felt the blood drain from her face as she turned quickly back to the road and pressed her spine against the seat. 'It's not ten thousand feet,' she whispered. 'It's ten million.'

'It's probably more like three thousand,' Grant said agreeably. 'We won't need oxygen masks after all.'

It was a joke, she knew. But, like all good jokes, it held a kernel of truth. The air did seem different here, now that she thought about it. She took a deep breath. Was it thinner? No. Not really. What it was, was cleaner. Sharper. It had a tang, like—like pine.

For the first time, she lifted her eyes to the mountains rising all around them. The trees—pine, for the most part—were a deep, deep green, a colour that mirrored that of the emerald on her finger, and they pierced a sky that was a shade of blue she could not recall ever having seen before, unless in a child's box of crayons.

Beautiful, she thought.

'Yes,' Grant said softly, 'it is, isn't it?'

Hannah swung towards him. 'I didn't say——'

'You didn't have to.' He gave her a quick smile, then looked back at the road. 'That catch in your breath said it all.'

'What catch in my breath?'

'There's a soft little sound you make when something pleases you.' His fingers flexed lightly on the steering-wheel. 'I think the first time I noticed was the night we bought Brian.'

'Brian?' she said, staring at him.

He grinned. 'Brian the Lion, remember?'

'Oh. Well, that was——'

'You make the sound when I kiss you, too.'

Colour rushed to her cheeks. 'That's ridiculous,' she snapped. 'And you're wasting your time if you think that kind of talk's going to——'

'The only thing I think is that we have to give ourselves a chance, Hannah. That's why I've made these arrangements, so that you and I——'

'There is no "you and I",' she said curtly. 'There's only a piece of paper no court in the world would hold me to. And you know it.'

He said nothing for a long time. When he spoke again, his voice was clipped.

'You keep forgetting that other piece of paper, the one that says we're husband and wife.'

Hannah stiffened. 'That one is meaningless, too.'

'Stop playing the innocent.' Grant's voice was iron-hard and unforgiving. 'You went into this with your eyes wide open—and, if you saw only what you wanted to see, you've no one to blame but yourself.'

She glared at him, but said nothing. What could she say? It was hard to admit, but he was right.

How could she have thought Grant would have agreed to a celibate relationship? He was a virile man, in the prime of his life. Had she ever stopped to think about what he was supposed to do for the time they lived out their sham of a marriage?

It didn't take much imagination to think of what the marriage would have been like if it had gone as she'd assumed. Grant would have lived a discreet private life, quite separate from the one he shared with her. He'd have had affairs, come home smelling of another woman's perfume...

A dull knot of pain lodged in her breast. She turned her head to look at him from under the shelter of her downcast lashes, her gaze running over the straight nose, the firm mouth and chin, drifting to the dark hair that brushed the collar of his cotton shirt. Her fingers curled into her palms as she remembered the silken feel of it under her hand—and suddenly she knew that she could not have survived hearing him come in late at night, knowing that he'd been...

The car coasted to a halt at the side of the road. 'Look,' Grant said quietly.

Hannah did, turning her face up to follow his pointing finger, eager to do anything to dispel the sudden clenching of her heart. A shadow swept towards them, borne on the wind, silent and almost supernatural.

'It's a golden eagle,' Grant said, answering Hannah's unspoken question. He shaded his eyes with his hand, watching as the eagle soared higher and higher until it was lost in the sun, and then he gave a deep sigh. 'Hell, don't you wish you had wings?'

Hannah's throat constricted. Yes, she thought, oh, yes, I do wish I had wings. I would fly away home, where I'd be safe...

Safe? From what? She knew Grant wouldn't hurt her. He wouldn't force a woman to submit to him. A woman would go to him eagerly, her eyes and arms open, her mouth parted for his kisses, her breasts hard and aching for his caress.

'There it is.'

She stared at him, too stunned by the images in her head to speak.

'The house,' he said, and now she could hear the excitement in his voice. 'There it is, Hannah. Just ahead.'

It stood in graceful solitude on a cliff above them, backed by the deep green of the mountain and looking out over the valley thousands of feet below. The house was white stucco with a red-tiled roof and red shutters, and Hannah knew she had never seen a more beautiful place.

It was, just as Grant had promised, the perfect honeymoon hideaway.

'Hannah?' Grant cleared his throat. 'Be honest. How does it look to you?'

She looked from the house to him. Like a dream, she thought, like the perfect place to be alone with the man you adore.

'Tell me what you think.' He reached out and smoothed a strand of dark hair from her cheek. 'Do you like it?'

Still, she said nothing. A month, she thought, four long weeks alone in this perfect place with Grant.

'I want you to like it,' he whispered. 'Hannah?'

The icy grasp of fear clutched at her chest, fear not of the man beside her but of the unknown that lay ahead. She pulled back sharply, away from the comforting warmth of his hand.

'Please.' She drew a trembling breath. 'Let's go back.'

'Hannah. Hannah, listen——'

'Don't force me to stay with you, Grant. Let me go. Let me out of this—this nightmare.'

Their eyes met, hers filled with pleading, his grey and hooded. Then, slowly, a cold smile angled across his mouth.

'You're breaking my heart,' he said sarcastically, and the car shot ahead.

The housekeeper and cook introduced themselves, then withdrew discreetly, leaving Grant and Hannah to explore the house themselves. Vivid Mexican tilework covered the floors; hand-woven blankets hung on the white-washed walls. The rooms were spacious and cool with their shutters drawn against the afternoon sun. They all opened on to a flower- and greenery-filled atrium where a miniature waterfall splashed over moss-covered stones into a pool designed to look as if it were set in a rocky hillside.

There were four bedrooms, each spacious and with its own private bath.

'Which do you prefer?' Grant asked.

More than ever, it seemed imperative to choose the one furthest from his.

'I'm not sure,' Hannah said carefully. 'What about you?'

'The one at the other end of the house seems fine.'

She nodded. 'I—I think I like this one,' she said, choosing the one they were in. Their eyes met. 'All right?'

'Fine. I'll bring in the luggage. Why don't you see if the cook's made preparations for lunch?'

She did as he'd suggested, and then she strolled through the atrium and pretended to look at the flowers, when all she was really trying to do was keep away from Grant. Something had happened in those last moments in the car, but what? She felt as if she'd touched her hand to an electric socket, felt the threatening tingle of power emanating from it before snatching her fingers away just in time.

'*Señora*?' Hannah looked up. The housekeeper was standing in the dining-room doorway, smiling politely. 'I have unpacked your things, *señora*. I hope I have put them away to your liking.'

Hannah nodded. 'Thank you. I'm sure whatever you've done is fine.'

'The *señor* asks me to tell you that he will join you for lunch in a few moments.'

Hannah touched the tip of her tongue to her lips. 'I—I'm not very hungry,' she said. 'The heat—the long drive...' Her voice trailed off. 'Would you please tell the *señor* that I've gone to take a nap? Tell him—tell him I'll see him later.'

Safe inside her room, she lay on the bed and stared up at the ceiling. Anger had propelled her through the last few hours, but it had suddenly drained away, leaving her with a hollowness deep inside. She felt vulnerable, even frightened, as if her world were about to turn upside-down.

There was a light knock at the door.

'Hannah?' The door opened and Grant stepped into the room. Hannah scrambled up against the pillows. 'Estrella says you're ill.'

She shook her head. 'Not ill. Just—just a little tired.'

'Would you like me to get you anything?'

'Nothing, thank you.'

'Some aspirin, perhaps. Or coffee?'

Hannah shook her head again. 'I just want to be alone.'

Grant's mouth twisted. 'Forgive me,' he said tightly, and the door swung shut.

She closed her eyes and lay there for a long time, deliberately trying to empty her mind of thought, but it was impossible. She felt as tense as a coiled spring. After a while she rose, walked to the window, and cracked the shutters.

The atrium was deserted in the afternoon heat. Hannah's gaze went to the pool. It looked cool and inviting, and she thought of how good it would feel to slip into the water and work off some of the restless energy dammed up inside her.

Quickly, she crossed to the dresser. Estrella had put her things away carefully, lingerie in the top drawer, cotton sweaters in the second—and swimsuits in the third. Hannah lifted out a white one, a bikini that was modest by current standards but still more revealing than any suit she'd ever owned.

'You'll look gorgeous in it,' Grant's sister had insisted.

She looked at herself in the mirror. What she looked was half-naked, but what did that matter? She would have the pool to herself.

She left her bedroom quietly. The flagstone floor of the atrium was warm against her bare feet; when she slipped into the water it seemed like silk against her skin. She swam endless laps, until finally she felt the dullness of exhaustion creep into her bones, and she climbed out of the pool to sink on to a lounger.

The sun was hot. Very hot. After a moment, Hannah closed her eyes.

... hands stroking across her, their touch light but exciting. 'Hannah.' Hands turning her over, drifting on her skin. Breath whispering against her hair, lips cool and sweet against her own. 'Hannah, sweetheart.'

'Hannah.'

'Mmm.' Sighing, she let the hands raise her up. She lifted her arms, curved them around the strong, masculine neck, let her fingers curl into the silken hair...

'Hannah. Hannah, wake up.'

Her eyes flew open. Grant was seated on the lounger beside her, holding her in his arms. His torso was sun-hot, naked against hers, his face so close that she could feel his breath on her cheek.

'Grant?' she whispered.

He smiled just a little. 'Yes.' His voice was soft and deep. 'You were dreaming.'

She swallowed drily. She felt as if she'd slept days instead of hours. 'I must have fallen asleep.'

His arms tightened around her. 'What were you dreaming about?'

Their eyes met. I was dreaming about you, she thought, about you, Grant...

'Nothing special,' she said carefully.

'Really?' He smiled into her eyes. 'Then why were you making that little sound?'

She was too confused to pretend she didn't know what he was talking about.

'I don't know,' she said, 'I was just dreaming, and—and...' She fell silent. He was too close to her, much too close. His skin smelled faintly of sun and sweat, a scent more heady and sensual than any ever created by a chemist for a men's cologne.

She took a steadying breath and pasted a smile to her face.

'I was dreaming that—that I was drinking a tall glass of iced water,' she said with a little laugh.

'I can make that dream come true.' He smiled and leaned away from her. When he turned around, there was a tall, frosted glass in his hand. 'Will lemonade do?'

The breath rushed from her lungs. 'Oh, yes,' she said. 'It'll do very nicely. Thanks.' She drank half the glass. 'Just what I needed,' she said brightly.

'Yes.' His hand brushed hers as he took the glass from her and put it on the table. 'I should have warned you. The sun's much stronger here than it is back home.'

Hannah nodded. Why did he keep sitting beside her? Why didn't he get up and sit on one of the other loungers, or slip into the pool?

She ran her tongue across her lips. 'Have you—have you been into the pool yet?'

'No, not yet.'

'Well, you should try it. The water's wonderful, very cool and—and...'

She was babbling like an idiot. It was his fault, not hers. It was disconcerting to have him sit so close to her, to have to watch the way his dark lashes fanned against his cheeks when he looked down, to have to see the play of muscle in his shoulders.

Hannah swung her feet to the flagstone floor. 'I guess I'll go inside now. I——'

'Come into the pool first.'

She looked up at him as he got to his feet. Her throat went dry. How beautiful he was! She had thought that this morning, when she'd seen him standing by the window wearing a towel; now, in a black Spandex suit, she could see even more of his body, see the narrow male hips, the washboard belly, the rounded convexity that was his manhood.

'Hannah?' She looked up at him. 'You're all flushed,' he said softly.

'Grant——'

'It's the heat,' he said. 'The sun.' He smiled and held his hand out to her. 'Take a swim and cool off before you go inside. You'll feel better.'

She put her hand in his and stood. Nothing would make her feel better, she thought dizzily, nothing but getting out of this house. But she let him draw her to the rocky steps that led down into the pool, and into the water.

'You can let go,' she said with a quick smile when the water was at her waist. 'I know how to swim.'

'Come in a little deeper,' he said softly, and he led her to where the rocky overhang formed a ledge over which water tumbled into the pool.

The water lapped softly at her breasts as he led her under the coolness of the waterfall.

'There.' He smiled. 'Isn't that nice?'

It was. But it seemed a mistake to tell him so—and yet wouldn't it be petty to do anything less?

She smiled, too. 'Yes. Very.'

'Your hair's getting wet,' he said.,

She laughed, surprising even herself. 'I don't mind,' she said, tilting her head back and closing her eyes. Grant had been right; the water did feel good. It felt wonderful against her heated skin.

'Hannah.' She opened her eyes. Grant was watching her, and when she saw his face her breath caught. His eyes were like obsidian, his mouth was a slashing line in his taut face. 'Hannah,' he said again, and he reached out one hand, very slowly, and ran it down her wet hair to her throat.

She swallowed hard. 'Don't. Please.'

'Do you know how beautiful you are?' he whispered. His fingers traced a pattern over her wet skin, skimmed across the rise of her breasts.

'Grant,' she whispered.

She wanted to tell him not to do this, but she couldn't. Her heart was racing as if she'd just climbed the mountain on foot. His fingers felt like tiny flames as they traced a path down her hip, and she felt a need building inside herself, a need that seemed stronger than her determination to stop him.

'I've wondered what you look like naked,' he said, his voice very soft, so soft she could barely hear it. 'I've imagined your body, the fullness of your breasts.' She gave a little gasp as his hand brushed across her bosom; she felt the instantaneous lift of her nipples and saw, in the swift darkening of his eyes, that Grant had seen it, too. 'I've pictured the sweet curve of your hips, the slight rounding of your belly...'

Hannah began to tremble. 'Don't,' she whispered, 'oh, don't...'

Grant stepped closer. His hands went to her hips, curved around her, cupped her buttocks.

'I lie awake at night, thinking of what it will be like when we make love the first time.' A moan whispered from her throat. His hands pressed lightly against her, urging her to him, and she came willingly, moving to him until their bodies touched. 'Will your thighs open for me?' His voice dropped until it was like thick, liquid honey. 'Will you wrap your legs around me and cry out when I enter you?'

Hannah swayed and his arms went around her, one hand dropping to the small of her back, bringing her tight against him. The hardness of his erection pressed into her belly.

'Hannah.' His breath whispered against her skin as he kissed the pulse racing at the hollow of her throat.

When his mouth found hers, she could not stop herself from kissing him back with wild, abandoned passion, her mouth open, her hands clinging to his shoulders. It was he who ended the kiss, putting her from him, holding her until her lashes lifted heavily from her flushed cheeks.

She looked at him. He was not smiling with a knowing triumph as she was afraid he might be; he was watching her instead with a look she could not define. Did he know that he could take her now if he wanted to, here, under the sky, with the sun beating down and the water surrounding them like warm silk?

After a long time, his hands fell away from her and he stepped back.

'Dinner in an hour,' he said, very calmly, as if what had just happened had been nothing but a dream.

It was as if she had been set free of a conjurer's spell. Hannah turned and dived under the water. She surfaced when she reached the edge of the pool, hoisted herself up, and then, without once looking back, made her way swiftly to her room and locked the door after her.

'Oh, God,' she whispered.

She knew he'd tried to seduce her—and he'd damned near succeeded.

She made her way unsteadily to the bathroom, stripped off her suit, and stepped into the shower. She turned the spray on full, tipped her head back, and let the cold water beat down on her face and body.

How would she manage four weeks of this? Grant was a master of a game that was new to her. She was susceptible to him, and he knew it.

She turned off the water and stepped on to the tiled floor. Being susceptible was one thing. Being a fool was quite another. Her mouth tightened as she wrapped herself in an oversized towel. How did that old saying go?

Fool me once, shame on you. Fool me twice, shame on me.

There wouldn't be a third time.

He was waiting in the garden when she came outside. She was wearing a lemon-yellow dress and matching high-heeled sandals; she'd brushed out her hair and she had a cool smile on her face.

The smile almost failed her when she saw him, standing tall and dark in a white dinner-jacket and frilled shirt, but then, there was no point pretending he wasn't handsome.

He was. But what did that mean to her?

The table was set with candles and fine china. Soft music drifted from hidden speakers.

The overture to Attempt Number Three begins, she thought, and she took a little breath, then put her head up and strolled briskly towards him.

'Hannah.' He smiled. 'You look lovely.'

'Thank you.' She took the glass of wine he held out and moved past him towards a bed of scarlet trumpet-flowers. 'These are spectacular,' she said, as if talking about flowers were what they'd done the last time they'd seen each other.

Grant didn't miss a beat. 'I'll bet the hummingbirds think so, too.'

She turned in surprise. 'Hummingbirds?'

He nodded. 'Sure. They're drawn to the colour red. There are probably half a dozen different varieties in this part of Mexico. A few years ago, when I was in Arizona...'

It was the start of a free-ranging conversation that at first made her suspicious, then confused, but eventually it was so fascinating that she forgot to be anything but interested.

They moved from hummingbirds to films, from films to books. Grant had an opinion on everything, which didn't surprise her. What did surprise her was the way he was willing to listen to her viewpoint, to concede that there might be another way of looking at things.

He was charming and attentive, and when, at midnight, he smiled and said that it was late, she was almost reluctant to agree.

But she was tired; she was yawning even as she got to her feet.

Grant smiled apologetically. 'I've kept you up too late,' he said. He put his arm lightly around her shoulders. 'Come on. We'll call it a night.'

She looked up at him, and all at once she remembered what she had for the past hours forgotten.

'You don't have to walk me to my room.'

'Don't be silly.' He smiled. 'It's not as if I have to go out of my way to do it.'

She let him lead her to the door. She walked stiffly, holding herself so that their bodies didn't touch. She was ready for what would surely come next—but not for what actually did.

Grant put his hands on her shoulders and dropped the lightest of kisses on her forehead.

'Goodnight, Hannah,' he said. He reached past her, opened her door, and gently put his hand in the small of her back. And, just like that, he was gone.

Hannah stood in the darkness while she tried to get her bearings. Was he really going to leave it at that? Yes. Apparently he was; she could hear the sound of his retreating footsteps.

Well, well, well. She kicked off her sandals, then unzipped her dress. It had been easier than she'd expected.

Moments later, face scrubbed free of make-up, wearing a T-shirt and her panties rather than going through the foolishness of putting on the nightgown Sally and the other girls had insisted on giving her, she climbed into bed and fell into a sound sleep.

She came awake slowly, shivering in the unexpected chill of a night breeze drifting in through the opened shutters. She sighed, tossed back the blankets, and padded to close the window, but when she reached it she froze.

A figure stood in the atrium, lit by the underwater lights of the pool. Grant, still dressed as he had been hours ago, in dinner-jacket and black trousers, stood staring at the shifting patterns in the water. There was something in the line of his shoulders that made her heart stop beating.

She did not know why she went to the door and opened it. Perhaps it was enough that it was night, that everything had the faint shimmer of illusion.

Her bare feet whispered across the flagstones. She stopped when she was at some distance from him and called his name softly.

He didn't turn, didn't seem surprised at her presence. His shoulders lifted, then fell, and she heard him sigh before he spoke.

'It's all right, Hannah. Go back to bed.'

'Grant—what's the matter?'

He shook his head. 'Nothing. I just couldn't sleep.'

She knew now what she'd seen in him when she'd looked out of her window. There was weariness in every line of his body, and it touched her heart.

She took a step forward. 'Can I do anything?'

'Can you...?' He laughed, although it didn't really sound like a laugh at all. 'Just go back to bed. I didn't mean to wake you. I—I won't disturb you any more.'

She went to him and reached out, then drew back her hand without touching his.

'If you—if you want to sit and talk for a while——'

'Talk?' He spun towards her; his tie was undone and the top buttons of his shirt were open. 'Talk?' His mouth twisted. 'Dammit, Hannah, I've had enough of talking.'

If only I could see his face, she thought, if only I could see what's in his eyes.

'I only want to help...'

'Then go to bed!'

'Is it——?' She swallowed. 'Is it because you're upset about us?' He didn't answer, and she moved closer. 'I didn't mean what I said,' she whispered, 'about—about prostituting myself. I mean, we misunderstood each other, that's all. I know you didn't——'

She cried out as he caught hold of her. 'You little fool,' he muttered, 'don't you understand?'

'I do. That's what I'm trying to tell you. No one has to know what went wrong between us, Grant. We can say we——'

'I thought I could do this,' he whispered. His hands slid to her throat, then to her face. 'I thought I could bring you here, keep my hands off you—hell, I thought I could court you——'

'Court me?'

'Yes, dammit. Court you, so it wouldn't come as such a goddamned shock when I took you to my bed.' His eyes swept over her face. 'I wanted to give us time, to give *you* time... but I can't!'

Hannah felt breathless, as if the air were being drawn from her lungs.

'I know you want me as much as I want you,' he said, 'but—— '

'You're wrong,' she started to say, but he shook his head.

'You don't have to say anything, Hannah. I know now that I'll never be able to change your mind.' He stuffed his hands into his trouser pockets, then turned his back to her. 'I've gone about this whole business with all the grace of a bull in a china shop, and I want you to know—I want you to know, I'm sorry.'

She took a step forward. Was he really apologising?

'You're free to leave,' he said. He took a breath. 'It's over.'

'Over?' she whispered.

'Yes.' He nodded. 'This is—it was a mistake.' His shoulders stiffened. 'We'll go home tomorrow.'

Tears of relief came to Hannah's eyes. It *was* over, really over. He was releasing her from her obligations, cancelling the contract.

'Just go back to your room,' he said.

'Grant——'

'Dammit, go!' He swung towards her, and his eyes met hers. 'I still want to make love to you, and if I start...' He swallowed, the sound audible in the silence. 'I won't stop,' he said fiercely. 'Not tonight.'

A hush seemed to fall over the garden. She could walk away from him. He had no hold on her any more...

Her head understood. But her heart was sending a different message. Go to him, it said with every beat. Now that he's given you a choice, you can go to him with your head held high. Go to him, Hannah. It's what you want, what you've always wanted...

'Then don't stop,' she said, and she was in his arms, her mouth open and hungry against his, giving now that she was free to give, taking what she had for so long wanted.

'Hannah,' he whispered, his mouth at her throat.

She could hear the question in his voice and she gave the only answer she could, clasping his head in her hands, dragging his mouth down to hers, kissing him with a passion that could no longer be controlled. Grant whispered her name and swung her into his arms.

Moonlight laid an ivory path across the flagstones to her room. He carried her to the bed and laid her down, and she watched as he pulled off his clothing.

Her hands moved over him, learning the satiny texture of his skin, the roughness of his hair, the hardness of his muscles. She lifted her arms and he drew away her T-shirt, then her panties, and then he was beside her, his mouth on her breasts and on her belly.

Suddenly she felt him tremble against her.

'Hannah,' he whispered.

'Yes,' she sighed, 'oh, please, yes.'

She arched to him as he entered her, meeting each deep thrust with joy and with an abandon she had never dreamed she possessed, so that before he called out her name and exploded within her she was already soaring up and up, shattering into thousands of tiny pieces in the blackness of the Mexican night.

An eternity later, Grant gathered her to him, stroked her hair, kissed her mouth.

'My wife,' he whispered, and Hannah turned her face into the crook of his shoulder and let her head know what her heart had long ago understood.

She was in love with Grant. It was why she'd wanted him so desperately yet tried so hard to deny the wanting. She loved him—and there was absolutely no future to it. Their marriage had ended before it began.

Only the formalities of its legal dissolution lay ahead.

CHAPTER ELEVEN

SUNLIGHT pierced the latticed wood of the bedroom shutters, striping the room in pale gold. Silence lay across the pool and the atrium, broken only by the chatter of the brightly feathered *periquitos* in the deep pine forest that rose behind the house.

Hannah lay dreaming in Grant's arms. In her dream, she wore a long white gown and carried a nosegay of pink tea-roses and baby's breath. She was walking on a carpet of pale green leaves, moving slowly towards the tall, dark figure of a man. His back was to her, she could not see his face, and yet she knew he was waiting for her. Knowing it sent a shudder of excitement through her.

Her breathing quickened, and she murmured in her sleep.

'Grant.' Her voice trembled in the still air.

The man turned and smiled. 'My wife,' he said, and her heart lifted.

A smile came to her lips, and her lashes fluttered open. She lay very still, struggling to get her bearings in a room that was totally unfamiliar, in a bed that was not her own.

She was in Grant's arms.

And she remembered.

This was where she had been all through the night, safe and warm in the arms of the man she adored—the man she would never see again, after this day ended.

She closed her eyes, letting her senses confirm what she already knew. She lay close in the curve of his arm, her head against his shoulder, her hand curled against his chest. Gently, so that she would not wake him and begin these last, tortured hours any sooner than necessary, she shifted her body until her mouth was pressed lightly to his skin, then inhaled his clean, masculine scent. Her hand opened, the fingers splaying into the soft, dark hair that whorled across his chest; the strong beat of his heart travelled through her fingertips and blended with her own.

Everything about the night had been so new. Her own unexpected passion, the feel of him moving within her, the tastes and textures of his skin—and yet she felt as if she had awakened here, in his arms, every morning of her life.

A sad little smile twisted across Hannah's lips.

'Who knows what love is?' Sally had sighed once.

'Not me,' Hannah had said with a quick laugh.

But she knew now. Love was finding the one man in the world who made you feel complete. It was awakening in his embrace for the very first time and realising that you had, at last, come home.

Hannah lifted her hand to Grant's face, touched his lips lightly with her fingers. A lump rose in her throat, and she rolled on to her back and laid her arm across her eyes.

She had been better off before she'd learned that love was real, that it wasn't just a word invented by poets and starry-eyed romantics. She understood the whole truth now.

It was possible to love without being loved in return.

Grant did not love her and he never would. It was as simple and as painful as that. He was a man for whom love could never be anything but a trap; it had been that shared belief that had brought them together and now, whatever she did, she could not tell him she'd been wrong, *they'd* been wrong.

Love wasn't a trap, it was a key—a key to happiness. Grant would laugh at her naïveté or, even worse, look at her with pity in his eyes and ask her what she was talking about.

As it was, she'd come close to giving herself away during the night.

'My beautiful, insatiable witch,' he'd whispered against her mouth once when she'd gone eagerly into his arms and let him take her on that dazzling journey to the stars again.

She'd ached with the fierce need to clasp his face in her hands, to whisper that she loved him as she'd never loved any man and that it was that, not magic or sex, that made her so hungry for his possession.

Hannah sighed. But she'd known better than to do that. Experience had honed her sense of self-preservation. As it was, she had left herself far too exposed. For years, she'd thought that the collapse of her first marriage had been the worst pain she'd ever endure, but now she knew that there could be something that would hurt her much, much more, the pain that would come of offering Grant her love and having him reject it.

And that moment, that truth, would come sooner or later, if she let their affair continue, she was certain of it. It was one thing to spend a night choking back the words she longed to whisper, but to do it night after night, day after day, for as long as Grant wanted her, would be impossible.

It was just a damned good thing they were no longer bound together by the terms of their damned contract.

Hannah stared at the play of light dancing on the ceiling. The minute Grant awakened, she would tell him she wanted to go home, make it clear that what had happened last night would never happen again. She was sure the news would not please him. During the night, he had spoken of the days—and the nights—that lay ahead.

'How would you like to drive down to Chichén Itzá and see the Mayan ruins?' he'd asked softly, while they lay in each other's arms and watched the moonlight dapple the ceiling. 'We can climb to the top of the temple of Kukulkán. They say you can see the edge of forever.'

That was when Hannah had begun the painful return to reality.

'No one can see that far,' she'd said after a moment.

Grant had smiled and kissed her forehead. 'My little pragmatist. How do you know until you try?'

Because there is no forever, not for us, she'd thought. She hadn't said it. She couldn't. It would have been too revealing. Instead, she'd closed her eyes tightly and admitted what her heart already knew, that this one night was all she could have with Grant. She had to give him up now, before loving him became as natural as breathing, before she stumbled and told him she never wanted to leave him, that she wanted to be his wife, his real wife, and never mind the stupid agreement that had once bound them together...

'Good morning, darling.'

Her eyes flew open. Grant was lying on his side, his head propped on his hand. He was looking down at her, a lazy, sexy smile on his mouth.

Hannah's heart turned over.

Why hadn't she got out of bed before he woke up?

'I was just having the nicest dream,' he said softly, 'about you being in my arms.' He reached out and traced the outline of her mouth with his fingertip. 'We were in a room filled with sunlight, and you were lying beneath me, your hair spread like dark silk across the white pillow.' He bent his head and kissed her mouth gently. 'You were asleep, and I woke you with a kiss.' Smiling, he stroked her hair from her face. 'And when you saw me you put your arms around my neck and said, "Good morning, darling."'

Hannah swallowed drily. She knew what was going to happen next; she could see it in the way his eyes were darkening to smoke, she could feel it in the heat spreading through her blood. And it could not happen, not if she was going to have the strength to tell him it was over.

'Say it,' he whispered.

She looked at him. 'Grant——'

'Not my name. Say, "darling".' He kissed her again, the tip of his tongue skimming lightly along the seam of her mouth. 'I want to hear you say it, Hannah.'

'Grant, please. It—it must be late.'

'Late?' He smiled and lowered his head to hers, so that his mouth just brushed her throat. 'Late for what?'

She closed her eyes as his lips moved against her skin. 'Late for—for breakfast. Estrella must be wondering——'

He looked up and laughed softly. 'Estrella's not wondering anything.' He took a strand of her hair between his fingers and brought it to his lips. 'She's wise enough to know that couples who come here to be alone aren't the most dependable guests in the world.'

'Really, wouldn't you like a cup of coffee?'

'Mmm. Coffee would be great.'

'Good. Then let me——'

'Coffee, a dozen eggs, and a pound of bacon. How's that sound?'

It was impossible not to smile. 'Who could eat so much first thing in the morning?'

'Me.' He chuckled softly. 'And you. You're supposed to have a voracious appetite this morning, Hannah.' He kissed her, and she could feel him smiling against her lips. 'Well, I guess I'll just have to make the sacrifice. A little exercise to start the day——'

She caught her breath as his hand moved on her. 'Please.'

'Please what?'

Please what, indeed? He was lying across her now, his mouth inches from hers, his hands in her hair. She could feel his heat, smell his scent, and, despite all her good intentions, her body was stirring, awakening to his.

He smiled. 'Say good morning to me properly, darling.'

'Grant, I don't——'

'Properly,' he whispered, and he gathered her to him and kissed her lips.

His mouth moving on hers was like a lick of flame, so hot against her lips, so sweet, urging her to open to him. And she couldn't. She couldn't.

Hannah twisted her face away. 'Don't.'

She felt the shock radiating through his body. He drew back and stared at her, and she felt her mouth begin to tremble.

'Don't,' she repeated.

When she tried to move away again, he let her. She sat up quickly, got to her feet, and threw on her robe. Silence filled the room.

'You can—you can shower first, if you like,' she said, her back to him.

'Hannah? What's the matter?'

'Nothing's the matter. I told you, it's late, and——'

He was behind her in an instant, his hands closing on her shoulders as he spun her towards him.

'Don't be ridiculous,' he said tightly. 'Something's wrong, and I want to know what it is.'

'I—I just said——'

'I know what you said. It's late. Estrella will be wondering why we haven't shown our faces. You want coffee.'

'That's right.'

His eyes searched hers. 'Now try giving me the real reason.'

Because I love you, she thought, because if you make love to me again I'll stay with you until you tire of me, and leaving you then will only break my heart more than it's breaking now.

'Well?'

She took a deep breath. 'I—I have something to tell you, Grant.'

Some of the tension eased from his face. He smiled a little, clasped her face and lifted it to his.

'Good. Because I have something to tell you, too.'

'Grant, please, you have to listen.'

'Don't you want to know what I have to say, Hannah?'

She sighed. 'All right. What is it?'

'Remember what we talked about last night? About going to Chichén Itzá?' He pressed a kiss to her temple. 'Well, I've a better idea. Let's not go there after all. Instead, let's fly to——'

'I don't want to go to Chichén Itzá or anywhere else,' she said sharply. 'That's what I'm trying to tell you.' Hannah drew a breath. 'I want to go home now. Today.'

'Go home?' His brows drew together. 'Back to San Francisco, you mean?' She nodded. 'But I thought you liked this house.'

'I do. I mean, the house is——' She looked into his puzzled face. 'It has nothing to do with the house, Grant. I just—I want to get back to my life.'

Uncertainty replaced puzzlement in his eyes. 'What's that supposed to mean?'

'It means exactly what I said.' Hannah flicked the tip of her tongue along her dry lips. 'This has been—it's been nice, but——'

'Nice?'

She could hear the sudden change in his voice, see the uncertainty in his eyes being supplanted by a smouldering anger.

'Nice?' he said again. His mouth twisted. 'Is that the best you can say about last night?'

She thought of what she longed to say—that it had been a night she would never forget—and knowing how close she was to making that impossible admission gave her the strength she needed to see this unhappy scene through to the end.

'Look, I know you probably thought we could—we could go on this way for a while, but——'

'But you're not interested.' The words were flat and cold. 'Come on, come on, spit it out; if that's what you're going to say, say it.'

'I'm not interested in having an affair with you, Grant. *That's* what I'm trying to say.'

His eyes locked on hers. 'I see.' There was a silence, and then a quick smile flashed across his face. 'Would you like to tell me why?'

'What do you mean, why? I just don't want to.'

Grant nodded. 'So you said.' His voice was low, very soft and steady. 'But I'd like to hear the reasons.'

Hannah stared at him. 'I don't have to explain myself to——'

'Yes.' She gasped as his hands tightened on her. 'Yes, you damned well do.' His mouth narrowed. 'You were incredible in my arms last night. And if you think I'm going to——'

Colour flooded her face. 'If you think *I'm* going to stand here and—and listen to a graphic description of—of my performance in your bed...'

She fell silent and stared at him, her face flushed, her breathing swift. He was impossible. Impossible! Here she was, her heart breaking at the thought of leaving him, and he was showing her that under the caring, gentle, passionate man he had been last night lay the heart of an egocentric, arrogant bastard, unwilling to let her out of his life until he was damned good and ready.

What she had to do was keep calm. Turning this into a confrontation wasn't going to make it any easier.

'Grant,' she said carefully, 'you're making more of this than it deserves. Just because I don't want to continue this arrangement——'

'And when did you reach that conclusion?'

This morning, she thought, as soon as I realised that staying with you even another day would only break my heart.

'I don't know, exactly.'

'You don't know, exactly.' His tone was ominously calm. 'Come on, Hannah, you can do better than that. Was it last night, when you came into my arms in the garden? Or at dawn, when you woke me by——'

She spun away from him. 'Stop it!'

'Why should I?' Grant grasped hold of her and forced her to face him. 'You wake up and announce you've had enough of this "arrangement" and that's that? You expect me to salute and say, terrific, Hannah, just let me find out what time the next plane leaves for home and——'

'My God!' Her flushed face turned up to his. 'Are you so damned used to getting things your own way that you can't handle having a woman think for herself?'

'Is that what this is? A blow for female liberation?'

'It's whatever you want to think it is. I've no intention of defending my decision.'

'And I told you, you'd damned well better!'

Their glared at each other, the only sound in the room the rasp of their breath, and suddenly Hannah felt as if the walls were closing in around her. She had to get out of this place with its faint scent of their lovemaking, had to have somewhere else to look besides Grant's angry face and the rumpled bed behind him.

Her throat worked as she swallowed. 'I'd rather continue this discussion over breakfast.'

His jaw tightened. 'That's the first intelligent thing you've said this morning.' He let go of her, turned, and strode into the bathroom door. 'I'm going to take a shower.'

The door slammed after him, hard enough to rattle the walls. Hannah threw off her robe as soon as she heard the water running and pulled on jeans and a cotton blouse, her fingers flying over the closures. Damn the man anyway! He was impossible.

And she was just as bad for still loving him.

She went still, took a breath, and looked into the mirror above the dresser.

Actually, he was making it easier for her. As long as he kept saying things to make her angry, she could leave him. But if he took her in his arms, whispered how much he wanted her...

She shuddered, walked quickly to the door, flung it open, and stepped into the bright morning light of the atrium.

The housekeeper had set a silver coffee-service on a small poolside table. Hannah poured herself a cup and drained off half of it. The coffee would clear her head. She refilled her cup, then sank into a chair. The thing to do was not let him put her on the defensive.

She looked up at the sound of his brisk footsteps. He looked at ease in faded denims and a navy shirt, but she knew immediately that his relaxed appearance was covering up a smouldering anger.

Her heart skipped a beat. She had to be strong.

'Now.' His words were clipped as he pulled out a chair, turned it around, and straddled it. 'What the hell is all this crap about not wanting to have an affair with me?'

She wanted to laugh. So much for worrying that he might try and kiss her into submission. Well, he had always been blunt. It was probably just as well he'd decided to be that way now.

'It's how I feel,' she said quietly. 'I'm sorry If I misled you into thinking anything else.'

His mouth hardened. 'Are you.'

It was not a question, but she accepted it as such.

'Yes. Last night, when you talked about staying on——'

'Did it amuse you? My planning the future, while you were planning your escape?'

Hannah's mouth trembled. What future? she wanted to say, but she knew better than to give herself away.

'It's foolish to put it that way, Grant. I'm not "escaping" anything. I just want to get back to San Francisco so I can get——'

'—back to your life. Yes. A charming phrase. But what does it mean?'

'I should think it's obvious what it means. I need a job, and a place to live.'

'A return to your much coveted independence,' he said coldly.

'Yes. That's right.'

'And you don't want to have an affair with me. Let's not leave that out.' He rose and poured himself a cup of coffee. 'Didn't anyone ever tell you it's polite to wait for an invitation before you turn it down?'

'What's that supposed to mean?'

'You gave me your decision even before I'd asked you anything.' He gave her a chill smile above the rim of his cup. 'But then, you always were most perceptive, Hannah.'

Her face flushed. 'Come on, dammit! I'm not a fool. I know what you have in mind.'

'Amazing, isn't it, how you always seem to know what I'm thinking?'

She stared at him, at the unyielding grey eyes and harsh mouth. 'That's hardly true,' she said, her voice shaking just a bit. 'I'd never have got myself into this mess in the first place if I did.'

His teeth flashed in a cold smile. 'I take it you're referring to our marriage.'

'Yes. If I'd known what you expected of me, I'd—I'd——' She broke off and turned her back to his chill stare. 'Look, this is all beside the point. I want to go home. End of story.'

'You mean, if you'd known I expected you to behave like a woman and not a machine, you'd never have agreed to marry me.'

'What about what I expected?' Hannah swung around, glowering.

'Oh, I know what you expected, Hannah.' His voice was like silk. 'You thought you'd get everything and give nothing in return, that you could have all the benefits of the arrangement without participating in it.'

'I didn't want an "arrangement", damn you!' Tears rose in her eyes.

'Of course not. Why would you want to be reminded that there are a woman's needs and desires tucked away inside that block of ice you call a heart?'

Hannah slammed down her cup. 'Now I understand. The great Grant MacLean thinks he awakened my libido, and now he expects to be properly thanked.' She rose to her feet. 'Well, I've got news for you. You didn't awaken anything. What happened last night had—had nothing to do with you.'

'Didn't it?'

His voice was ominously soft, but Hannah was beyond hearing anything but her own anger and pain. She rose to her feet and faced him, her face pink, her hands on her hips.

'You're right,' she snapped. 'I suppose I do have certain needs. Who doesn't? You were just in the right place at the right time.'

He stepped forward swiftly and clasped her wrist tightly. She cried out as he twisted her hand up between them, until her fingers were spread before her eyes.

'What do you see?' he grated through his teeth.

Hannah stared at him. 'Let go!'

'Answer the question!' His head shot forward. 'Tell me what you see.'

'I don't——'

'A ring. A circle of yellow gold.' His smile was frigid. 'And I'm the man who put it there.'

'Much to my regret,' Hannah snapped.

Grant laughed. 'Such sweet words for a bride to whisper to her husband after their first night together, darling.'

'Stop this nonsense! You are not my husband.'

'I am whatever the hell I say I am,' he snarled. Their eyes met. 'And I say we're still married.'

Hannah stared at him. 'But you said—last night——'

'To hell with last night!' His words were taut with barely contained fury. 'I've had it with jumping through hoops.'

'What?'

His mouth narrowed. 'You're going to have to find yourself the best attorney money can buy if you want out of this marriage.'

'It's not a marriage,' she said quickly. 'You know that. It was an arrangement.'

Grant's face darkened. 'Tell it to the judge.'

He let go of her wrist, brushed past her, and stalked into the house without so much as a backward glance.

Hannah stared after him. How could she ever have deluded herself into thinking that she loved him?

CHAPTER TWELVE

AT LEAST Grant came to his senses long enough to agree that there was no point in staying in Mexico. It was a small victory, but by then Hannah was willing to take whatever she could get.

It took all her determination to sit silently beside him while they drove to the airport; she knew that any pleading, even any further show of anger on her part, would only deliver more control of her life into his hands. She had nothing to go home to: no job, no flat, no money. She was tied to him by a certificate of marriage and his insistence on holding her to a contract made in hell.

Once they were seated in the first-class cabin of the jet bearing them back to the States, he turned to her.

'I telephoned Marilyn,' he said crisply. 'I told her the same thing we'll tell anyone else who asks—that I was called home by unexpected business.'

Hannah stared straight ahead. 'Tell them what you like.'

'Just be sure you have the story straight, Hannah,' he said coldly.

She looked at him. 'I hardly think I'll be talking to anyone who gives a damn.'

'People will expect to see us together for the next few weeks,' He smiled tightly. 'After all, darling, technically, we'll still be on our honeymoon.'

Hannah glared at him. 'Only because you decided to extend it.'

'Yes.' A muscle knotted in his jaw. 'One of my many errors, and too late to do anything about now.'

'It's never too late,' she hissed. 'You're just afraid your damned ego will take a beating if——'

'There's nothing to discuss,' he said, his harsh voice cutting across hers. 'For the next few weeks you'll be seen in public with me, you'll entertain guests in our home——'

'If you try and—if you touch me,' she said in a shaky whisper, 'I promise you, you'll regret it.'

His mouth became a thin slash in his dark face. 'I already do,' he said coldly, and then he looked away from her, folded his arms across his chest, and laid his head back against the seat.

Hannah didn't answer. She hadn't meant to say that; it was foolish to let him see her fear. Besides, what was there to fear, anyway? She had never been afraid of him forcing himself on her and she still wasn't. The danger had been in his seducing her, but that was finished. She'd never tumble into his bed again. Never!

If only she had someone or somewhere to run to. But she'd kept to herself since her divorce; Sally was the closest she had to a friend, and she could never drag her into the middle of this disaster. Grant could be vengeful; he'd not hesitate to destroy anyone who came to her assistance.

He didn't want her, he never had, except in the terms of their contract. All this was an exercise of power, and the ache deep inside her that would not go away had nothing to do with caring about him. It was about—about hating him.

'*Madame*?' She looked up. The flight attendant was offering a brilliant smile along with a glass of champagne. 'What may I get you?'

My life as it was, before Grant MacLean took it over, Hannah thought.

'Nothing,' she said with a quick shake of her head, 'nothing, thank you.'

'Nor for me,' Grant said in clipped tones.

It was the last either of them spoke until their plane had landed.

* * *

Hannah knew that Grant lived in a large penthouse apartment. She had expected it to be elegant, even opulent. But, when the doors to the penthouse's private lift slid open, what she saw took her breath away.

An enormous marble entry-foyer stretched before her, illuminated by a glittering crystal chandelier that hung from a ceiling that stretched three storeys high. Hannah craned her neck up. Paintings hung on the walls, of a sort she'd only seen in galleries and museums, and above them rose the shadowy second- and third-floor balconies. She looked down again, to where a statue that looked suspiciously like a Brancusi stood in solitary splendour in the far corner.

'I trust you're not waiting for me to carry you across the threshold,' Grant said coldly.

Hannah took a quick step forward. 'I'm too tired to play games,' she said. 'If you'd just tell me where my rooms are...?'

'The master suite takes up the entire third level.'

She swung towards him. 'I said *my* rooms, Grant! You promised me I'd have my own quarters.'

His teeth bared in an unpleasant smile. 'I've changed my mind.'

'What do you mean, you've changed your mind? You can't possibly think I'd——'

'Good evening, sir.' Hannah turned. A manservant was striding towards them, smiling politely. 'Welcome home. And a special welcome to you, Mrs MacLean.'

Grant nodded. 'Hodges. How are things?'

'Very well, sir. Shall I take your luggage up?'

'Not mine,' Hannah said sharply. 'Take my things to the guest room, ple...' Her breath hissed as Grant's hand closed tightly on her arm.

'Take everything to my rooms,' he said through his teeth. 'My wife and I will be in the study. And we don't want to be disturbed.'

'I'm not going with you,' Hannah whispered fiercely, but Grant was half lifting her to her toes, hurrying her through the foyer, then through a pair of carved doors that swung shut after them with finality.

He swung her towards him. 'What the hell kind of a performance was that?' he demanded in tight-lipped fury.

'I am not sleeping in your bed,' Hannah said just as angrily. 'If you think, for so much as a minute, that——'

She cried out as his fingers dug into her flesh. 'But you are, my beloved wife. There's the matter of a contract to be adhered to, remember?'

Hannah flung up her chin. 'You cannot hold me to that ridiculous arrangement, and you know it!'

'No?'

'No! And if you try——'

'I told you, sweetheart, get yourself an attorney. And he'd better be a damned good one, because I'll fight him every step of the way!' Grant let go of her and stalked across the room. 'In the meantime, you'll obey the rules.'

'Rules?' She stared at him as he threw open the doors to a mahogany *secretaire*, revealing a built-in drinks cabinet. 'What rules?'

'Actually,' he said as he wrenched the top from a decanter, 'there's only one rule.' Amber liquid splashed into a cut-glass tumbler. He raised the glass to his lips and tossed half of it down. 'You will remember who you are——'

'A woman who wants her freedom! You'd better remember it, too.'

'You are my wife. And you will behave properly. At all times.'

Hannah laughed. 'What does that mean? Am I expected to curtsy?' She marched towards him. 'Or will a simple kowtow do?' Her jaw shot forward. 'You'll wait till hell freezes over before——'

'You will never, ever pull a scene like that one again.' Grant slammed his half-empty tumbler down and clasped her by the shoulders. 'Is that clear?'

'Why?' Hannah tossed her head. 'Is your poor ego so fragile that you can't face letting the world know that our marriage isn't a marriage at all?'

A fleeting darkness swept across his face. 'I keep telling you, I don't care what the world thinks.'

'Or is it because you refuse to admit that, for once in your life, you're not going to get what you want?'

The darkness came again, this time settling in his eyes. 'If I don't,' he said, after a moment, 'it won't be for lack of trying.'

Hannah flushed. 'Would you really stoop so low? Is getting your own way so important that you'd force me to sleep with you?'

His hands tightened on her. 'Damn you, Hannah,' he said fiercely, 'damn you to hell!'

He pulled her into his arms and his mouth fell on hers. His kiss was harsh, a reflection of anger, not desire. Hannah struggled against it, trying to twist her face away from his, but he thrust his hands into her hair and held her fast.

'Stop pretending you're made of ice, dammit! We both know you're not.'

He kissed her again, his mouth grinding against hers. She stood absolutely still, receiving the kiss as if she were made of stone, determined not to let him see how bleak her despair was.

This was the man who'd held her in his arms and made love to her with tenderness and warmth. This was the man she'd been fool enough to think she loved...

He let her go, pushing her from him, his eyes dark and cold. 'It seems I was right about you, Hannah,' he said. 'You're not a real woman at all.'

The words stabbed into her heart, but she didn't so much as flinch. Grant went on looking at her, and then he strode to the door and threw it open. 'Hodges!' he bellowed. 'Move my wife's luggage to the guest suite.'

Without so much as a backward glance he vanished up the stairs.

* * *

The days passed, and the weeks. Life fell into a routine. Hannah rose early, breakfasted in her rooms, then looked for ways to make the hours go by, but there were only so many art exhibitions and museums you could attend, especially when you had to feign interest to begin with. She had little interest in anything. How could she, when she lived like a prisoner, even if her prison was a beautiful penthouse filled with exquisite things?

Sally phoned once, and they met for lunch. But Sally's usual giggles had given way to a kind of awed nervousness, until finally Hannah threw down her napkin in disgust.

'For goodness' sake,' she said sharply, 'what's wrong with you?'

'Well—well, it's different now, isn't it? I keep thinking, she's not Hannah Lewis at all, she's Hannah MacLean. And——'

'That's nonsense. I'm still me, the same as always.'

'Sure,' Sally said, after a moment, 'the same as always.'

But they had not seen each other again. And that was just as well, Hannah knew, not because of any difference in status but because, sooner or later, the sharp-eyed Sally would surely have picked up on what Grant's sister had already noticed. They had only spent one evening with Marilyn and her husband, after Marilyn had cheerfully threatened to show up at the door unannounced if Grant and Hannah turned down one more invitation to dinner, but that had been enough for the other woman to sense that something was wrong between her brother and his bride.

'Grant can be a difficult man,' Marilyn said softly, as she and Hannah got Tommy ready for bed.

Hannah picked up Brian the Lion and stroked his mane absently as she groped for an answer, watching as Marilyn bent and pressed her lips to her son's tousled curls. Her throat constricted. Yes, she thought, you're right. Your brother only married me so he could have a child. And—and I would have loved to have had that child. His child. Grant's...

'Hannah?' Marilyn straightened and put her hand on Hannah's arm. 'Is there something wrong?'

Hannah forced a smile to her lips. 'No, nothing. We're just—we're just learning to live together. You know how it is.'

Marilyn nodded. 'So long as you love each other, everything will turn out fine.'

But we don't love each other, Hannah thought. He doesn't even like me. And I—I certainly don't—I don't...

Without warning, tears sprang to her eyes. She turned away quickly and wiped her palms across them. Grant, Grant, she thought...

And, as if her thought had summoned him, there he was, in the doorway. They stared into each other's eyes, and then Hannah lifted her chin, set her mouth, and swept past him.

'It's late,' she said. 'And I'm tired. I'd like to go home.'

It was the last they saw of Marilyn and her family. Grant was busy, he said, too busy to spend much time anywhere but at the office or in his study at home, but Hannah knew he simply wanted to avoid her. He was beginning to resent her intrusion into his life. He had married her for one purpose, and she was not fulfilling it. Despite the implied threats he'd made that first evening, he had not tried to force her into his bed.

All that kept him from letting her go, Hannah was certain, was his refusal to admit that he'd made a mistake in convincing her to marry him. She told him that whenever she could, each time ending with a plea that he put an end to their marriage.

His answer was always the same. 'I will, when I'm good and ready.'

And that would end it.

The only times they spoke cordially to each other were on those occasions when she had to go with him to a business dinner or play hostess to one in his home. She even had to endure the light pressure of Grant's arm around her waist, the smile that seemed warm but had no meaning, the light brush of his mouth against her cheek.

Aside from those evenings, their paths rarely crossed.

It was, she thought late one afternoon, as she stepped from the lift after another empty day, as if she had ceased to exist for him. And that was just fine with her. It meant that, any day now, Grant would call her into his study, fix her with that unnerving stare, and tell her that this impossible masquerade was over.

Which was what she wanted. Exactly what she wanted. Then why did the thought bring such a sense of despair?

'Mrs MacLean?'

'Yes, Hodges?'

'Mr MacLean phoned while you were out, madam. He said to tell you he'd be bringing some guests home for dinner.'

Hannah's face fell. Another artificially cheerful evening for important clients. She felt exhausted at the thought. It was getting harder and harder to smile and pretend for strangers.

'I've taken the liberty of speaking with Cook. I hope that's all right...?'

Hannah nodded. She had no hand in running this house. It was Grant's home, not hers; she was little more than a non-paying boarder.

'Yes, that's fine. Thank you. Did he say when he'd be here?'

'At seven, madam.'

That gave her plenty of time to shower and change, she thought as she entered her bedroom. To paint some life into her face, to slip into one of the expensive gowns that hung in her wardrobe—and to assume the role of the wife she would never be.

Her throat tightened. 'I can't do this any more,' she whispered into the silence of her bedroom.

But she would have to. The lie they were living would end when Grant chose to end it, and not a moment sooner.

Hannah came down the stairs at two minutes to seven, just in time to greet Grant and his guests as the lift doors opened. Her brows lifted a little when she saw Messrs Longworth, Hart and Holtz step forward, their wives on their arms.

'Hannah,' a chorus of male voices said, and they all clustered around, greeting her with hearty kisses on the cheek, while their wives eyed her and gave each other strange little smiles. Well, after all, Hannah thought, it wasn't every day one of the partners married his legal assistant. If only they knew...

'Hello,' she said pleasantly, after introductions were made. 'How lovely to see you all.' She peered past them to the lift doors, which had whisked shut. 'Where's Grant?'

'Riding up with the next batch,' Mrs Holtz said. There was another round of funny smiles as the women dumped their minks and sables into Hodges' arms. 'There were simply too many of us to arrive together!'

Everyone laughed harder than they should have, Hannah thought, but she went on smiling.

'I'm sure you know your way into the living-room. Why don't you go ahead and let Hodges serve you drinks? I'll wait here for the others.'

The men all started across the foyer, but Mrs Hart's breathless voice stopped them in their tracks.

'Oh, we'll wait with you,' she said—and just then the lift doors slid open, and everything grew still.

Stepping into the foyer were the primary members of the Hungarian delegation—but left behind in the lift, so that they took centre-stage, were Grant and Magda Karolyi, she clutching his arm and gazing up into his face with unconcealed adoration, he smiling down into hers.

'. . . and then,' Grant said into the silence, 'Stevens said, "Well, Your Honour, I would have brought them all into the courtroom, but I figured the place would get a little crowded. So I left them at home, in the fishbowl. But you're welcome to drop by and check for yourself, any time." '

Magda threw back her head and laughed, exposing perfect white teeth. 'Darling, that's absolutely marvellous! And, of course, you von the case!'

Grant smiled modestly. 'Of course.'

Magda giggled like a schoolgirl. 'How vonderful!' Her dark chocolate eyes glowed. 'Oh, it's so good to see you again, darling. You can't imagine how I've missed you.'

'Grant?' Hannah swallowed. 'Grant,' she said again, and the couple in the lift looked away from each other and stared at her as if she was the last person either of them had expected to see.

Grant recovered first. 'Hannah.' He smiled as he drew Magda forward. Hannah's heart missed a beat. He was smiling at her as he had done in the days when she was his assistant: pleasantly, politely—and impersonally. 'Hannah, you remember Magda, don't you?'

Hannah tore her eyes from him. 'Yes,' she said slowly. 'Of course.' She took a breath. 'How are you, Ms Karolyi?'

'Oh, you must call me Magda,' the blonde said. 'If you call me Ms Karolyi, then I must call *you* Mrs MacLean.' She gave Grant a sidelong glance from beneath impossibly long lashes. 'And vy should I spend the evening reminding myself that you are married to this beautiful man?'

Everyone laughed gaily, including Hannah. But her laugh began and ended a fraction of an instant too late, so that it hung in the air like a forgotten party balloon. After a moment, Mr Longworth cleared his throat.

'Well,' he said in a jolly voice, 'well, well, well. Have you told your wife what it is we're celebrating, Grant?'

Grant's smile was slow and knowing as he looked at Hannah. 'No,' he said softly, 'I haven't. But then,

Hannah's a bright girl, Charlie. I'm sure she's figured it out.'

Longworth launched into a little speech about finally concluding the Hungarian deal, but Hannah knew the truth. Grant's message had been clear. It was over. The charade he'd forced her into was finished. I'm tired of playing, Hannah, his eyes said. And I don't give a damn who knows.

Well, that was fine with her, she thought. But why the public announcement? What right had he to make her look like a fool? None of these people, not even the voluptuous blonde hanging on Grant's arm, was stupid. Something was happening; they knew it, just as Hannah knew that they were all waiting for her reaction.

Well, she thought grimly, they were in for a disappointment. She would be a lady. She would endure this evening, pretend complete indifference to what was going on under her nose. And at the night's end she would pack her things—her things, nothing Grant had bought her—and walk out with her head high.

She owed that much to herself.

Three hours later, as she began pouring coffee in the library, Hannah was ready to admit that her plan, though intellectually sound, wasn't working.

She couldn't seem to concentrate on anything but Grant and the woman who clung to him like a shadow, who was now seated close beside him on a small sofa far from everyone else. If it hadn't been for Hodges, Hannah's guests would have gone without drinks and food. And she had no idea why.

Why did she keep looking at Grant and Magda? It was like approaching the scene of an accident along the road.

I won't look, you told yourself.

But you did. You did, because you just couldn't keep from doing it, no matter how painful the result—just as she couldn't keep from looking towards those two heads, one dark, one fair, bent towards each other.

Grant wasn't just making a fool of her, he was making one of himself. Didn't he care? She knew what he always said, that he didn't give a damn what people thought, but surely...?

Magda's laughter tinkled across the room like a scale played on a poorly tuned piano. Grant laughed, too. He'd been laughing all night. Had he ever laughed so much before? Not with her, surely.

'...all *so* surprised!' Hannah blinked. Mrs Hart was smiling at her. 'Such a sudden thing, your marriage, wasn't it, dear?'

Hannah smiled stiffly in return. 'May I pour you some coffee?'

Grant was laughing again. If she tried, she could even pick up bits and pieces of his conversation.

'...and then the poor bastard said, "Where's my litigant?" Can you imagine?'

Magda chuckled sexily. 'Who could win against you, darling?' she purred. 'You are such a formidable man!'

Grant chuckled. 'Oh, I can think of times I'm a pushover,' he said.

Coffee slopped over Mrs Hart's cup and into the saucer. 'Sorry,' Hannah said.

'No!' Hannah could almost picture Magda batting her lashes. 'You, a pushover? Never, darling.'

'I am, for a beautiful woman,' Grant said.

'Oops!' Hannah smiled brightly at Mr Longworth. 'I'm so sorry! I didn't burn you, did I?'

The voices coming from the little sofa dropped until they were inaudible. Well, Hannah thought, Grant and Magda deserved each other. They were both of a kind, all looks and no heart. But Magda was in for a surprise. She was probably already picking the colour of her bridesmaids' dresses, but no one, not even a blonde with abundant cleavage, would ever get Grant to the altar once their divorce was—was——

'Sorry. I don't know what's wrong with me this evening. Here, let me blot that up...'

But she'd surely get Grant into her bed, and probably long before that divorce decree had even——

Hannah grabbed at a napkin. 'I'm so sorry!'

Grant was a man with a strong sexual appetite, and it was obvious he found Magda attractive. Attractive wasn't quite the word. He found her stimulating. Exciting. Just look at how he was practically purring as she leaned into him——

'Lord! I'm all thumbs tonight. Did I burn you? Good. Good. Let me just——'

Why was he letting her do that? Her breast was practically in the crook of his elbow...

Hannah sprang to her feet. 'I—I——' She stared wildly at the faces watching her, then reached down and snatched up the half-full cream pitcher. 'We need more cream,' she said. 'I'll just—I'll just go and...'

She rushed out the door, then stood in the shadows, shaking. Why? Why did it matter to her what Grant did with that woman? The answer came at once. She had told herself she wouldn't let his behaviour embarrass her, but it was doing exactly that. *He* was embarrassing her, when he was the one who ought to hang his head in shame. What if the people in that room knew the truth, that Grant had contracted with her for a child, that she'd refused his advances?

If they knew, they'd feel differently. By God, if Magda Karolyi knew the truth, *she'd* feel differently! No woman, not even this one, would make such stupid cow eyes at a man as cold-blooded, as self-centred, as heartless as Grant MacLean.

Magda's laughter rang out again. 'Oh, Grant, you are so charming!'

Charming? Hannah spun on her heel. 'Enough,' she said, as she marched into the library and straight for the little sofa. Someone reached out a hand but she brushed past it. 'Grant.' Her voice rang out, loud and clear in the sudden silence.

Grant looked up, still smiling at whatever Magda had been saying. 'Yes?' he said, a bit impatiently. 'What is it, Hannah?'

'What does Magda know about us?'

His brows drew together. 'What?'

The blonde leaned towards him, her breasts almost spilling from her dress. 'What is she talking about, darling?'

Grant smiled. 'Nothing to worry your lovely head about.'

'Nothing?' Hannah said sharply. She took a step forward. 'Nothing?' she repeated with barely suppressed rage.

'Oh, good,' Magda said, happily oblivious to what was going on, 'you have the creamer. I should like some, if you please.'

There was a moment of seemingly endless silence. Hannah could feel every eye in the room on her. A shiver of anticipatory pleasure coursed through her blood.

'Of course,' she said, very calmly, 'you can have it all.' And she up-ended the pitcher directly on to that overblown décolletage.

Magda shrieked, leaped to her feet, and began to sputter in Hungarian. 'You are a crazy woman!' she finally managed in English.

Hannah smiled. 'Indeed,' she said, and with her head held high she turned and marched from the room.

It wasn't until she was safely in her rooms that her composure crumpled. She fell back against the door. Lord! What had she done? Grant had not humiliated her half as much as she'd humiliated herself. She'd set out to salvage her pride, and instead she'd—she'd...

'Hannah?'

The knock at the door, and the determined sound of Grant's voice, were almost simultaneous.

'Go away,' she said.

'Open the door, Hannah.'

He sounded as if he might break it down. Hannah sighed, reached for the knob, and yanked it open.

'We've nothing to say to each other, Grant.'

He walked past her, surprisingly cool for a man who'd just endured such a nasty little scene.

'Our guests asked me to say goodnight.'

Her cheeks coloured. 'Did they?'

He peered at a painting on the wall as if he'd never seen it before. 'That was one hell of a performance you just gave.'

Hannah's chin lifted. 'If you or your—your lady-friend expects an apology——'

'I told Magda to buy herself a new dress and send you the bill.'

'Me?' Hannah laughed, although she didn't feel much like laughing. 'That was a waste of time, Grant. I couldn't afford to pay it—even if I wanted to.'

'Of course you can,' he said mildly. 'There's plenty of money in your account.'

'There's plenty of money in Hannah MacLean's account, you mean.' She strode past him to the bedroom, switched on the light and opened the wardrobe closet and pulled it open. 'But not in Hannah Lewis's,' she said, as she began tossing her things on the bed.

'What are you doing?'

'What does it look as if I'm doing?'

Grant shrugged and leaned back against the wall, his arms folded over his chest.

'There's no rush, Hannah. You don't have to get your things moved out tonight. It can wait till morning.'

Her throat constricted, although why should it? She'd known what he was doing, that he was telling her to get out of his life. And that was what she wanted, what she'd wanted all along.

'What can't wait until morning is an explanation.'

'There's nothing to talk about.'

His tone hardened. 'I want an explanation of what happened in that library.'

Hannah's face burned. 'I told you, I'm not going to apologise. Anyway, you made your point.'

'Did I?'

'Yes. But it wasn't necessary. You knew I wanted to end this—this marriage. You didn't have to—to...' Her voice broke. Dammit! She wasn't going to break down in front of him. And there was no reason. No reason at all.

'Hannah.' Grant's hands closed lightly on her shoulders. 'Hannah, turn around and look at me.'

'No.'

Slowly, gently, he turned her towards him. When she looked down, he put his hand under her chin and urged her head up.

'If you're glad our relationship is over, why are you so upset?' he asked softly.

'Why am I...? You—you humiliated me. You——'

'Is that the only reason?'

'Yes. Of course. I have my pride too, you know. You're not the only one...'

But he was. He was the only one, the only man she would ever love. She had loved him all along, despite the lies she'd told herself.

A sob burst from her throat.

'Go away,' she whispered. 'Grant, please, if you ever had any respect for me...'

'What I hoped,' he said, his hands framing her face, 'was that maybe you were upset because I'd made you jealous.'

'Jealous?' Hannah sniffed. 'Me? Why on earth would I be——?'

'I don't know,' he said, very softly. 'Maybe because you love me.'

His eyes were boring into hers. She wanted to look away from him, but how could she, when he was holding her face between his hands?

'This is ridiculous,' she said. 'If you think you can humiliate me more than—than I've already humiliated myself——'

He stopped her words with a gentle kiss. When he drew back, he was smiling.

'I'm even wondering if perhaps you love me as much as I love you.'

Hannah's eyes grew wide.

'Did you hear me, sweetheart? I love you. I love you as I never dreamed it possible to love anyone.'

Her heart skipped a beat, then began to race like an engine out of control.

'Grant,' she said shakily. 'Do you—do you mean it?'

'I don't even know when it happened. Maybe it was when you snatched that black nightgown out of my hands. Maybe it was when you served me a cup of the worst coffee any man's ever endured, or when you gave yourself to me that night, beside the pool.'

'But—but tonight...'

'Hell.' He shook his head. 'Tonight was the act of a desperate man. We couldn't talk without resorting to accusations. And you turned to ice when I tried to tell you how I felt before.'

'When?' Hannah breathed. 'When before?'

'That morning, in Mexico. I started to ask you to go with me to a little town where we could be properly married, without any nonsense about contracts or——'

'But that was why you'd asked me to marry you in the first place. So you could have a child.'

Grant sighed and rubbed his cheek against her hair. 'That's true. I'd thought about having a child on and off for a long time—but it was always in the abstract. Hell, having a child meant getting involved with a woman, and I'd no wish to do that ever again. But then you came along—and suddenly the idea of having a baby seemed very enticing.'

'But not too enticing.' She looked at him. 'You only wanted a marriage with a built-in divorce clause.'

'And so did you.'

Hannah nodded. 'I told myself it was the only arrangement that suited me——'

'Yes, darling.' He smiled. 'Neither of us was willing to admit we'd fallen in love.'

'I know in my heart that I'd never have agreed to marry you for any reason but love.'

Grant gathered her close. 'You do love me, then,' he said softly, and Hannah tilted her head up to him and smiled.

'Oh, yes,' she whispered. 'I knew it that night, in Mexico. When you set me free, I looked into my heart—and realised I'd loved you for a long, long time.'

'But if you knew how you felt, why did you want to end things?'

Hannah sighed. 'Once I knew I loved you, how could I have lived with you, then given you up when you tired of me?'

'Hannah, sweetheart.' Grant drew her close and kissed her. 'I'll never tire of you, not if we both live to be a hundred.'

Tears rose in Hannah's eyes; she smiled through them and looped her arms around his neck. 'Poor Magda. What must she think?'

Grant grinned. 'Don't feel sorry for her, love. She enjoyed herself tonight; I suspect she likes playing the role of sex goddess more in public than she's capable of performing it in private.'

'And your partners.' Hannah buried her face in his shoulder. 'And their wives. Just imagine what they must be saying.'

'Yup. They probably haven't had this much excitement in decades.' He laughed softly. 'We'll make it up to them, and to Magda, too, by inviting them all to our wedding. A real wedding, darling. You will marry me again, won't you?'

'Only if it means I get another wedding night.'

Grant smiled. 'Every night we spend together will be a wedding night, sweetheart, all the years of our lives.'

He bent to her and kissed her. When he drew back, Hannah sighed.

'What a pity,' she said. 'Here you had an evening all planned, and I spoiled it. Whatever will we do with the rest of the night?'

Grant swung her into his arms. 'Why don't I take you on a tour of the apartment?'

'But I've seen it.'

He gave her a long, dizzying kiss. 'You've never seen my bedroom, Mrs MacLean,' he whispered.

Hannah sighed. 'Mrs MacLean,' she murmured. 'What a lovely sound that has...'

'On second thought,' Grant said as he lowered her to the bed, 'let's start with a tour of this room. How does that sound, darling?'

'It sounds wonderful,' Hannah murmured.

And then neither of them said anything for a very long time.